# Roses are Red

CIANA SMOAK

# Contents

For all the girls who dream of being treated like a princess. There is someone out there who will.

# Chapter 1



If I see the colors red and pink one more time, I may just throw up. I never see so many stuffed animals and candy until this dreaded time of year. Aisles and aisles of brown bears and candy boxes with seasonal designs to celebrate this horrible holiday. Leave it to my sister to drag me in public where it's shoved in your face. I can barely escape it while watching my favorite reality TV shows after work. I swear If I see more loveable chocolate commercials, I may just sue for the manifestation of diabetes.

"Kayani, Fix your face, your grumpiness is showing." Kassiah says to me as she picks up a heart shaped box of chocolates for her daughter, Star.

"My face has a mind of its own." I say, looking up at the big fluffy dust collector holding a red heart with the words *I love you* written on the plush fabric. As if the dark gray oversized sweats, messy bun and constant frown on my face don't already exude grumpy. Only reason I came outside was because we said we were going to pick out my dress for my catch up dinner with Rosen. I didn't know we would be making a pit stop beforehand.

Kassiah walks over to me with a wide smile on her face, I can tell it's fake but it's something she wants me to mimic. I shake my head and turn back to the Valentine decorated candy boxes.

"Come on, let me see your pretty smile." She says, trying to get her face in my line of vision.

"No thank you, Kassiah." I say picking up a box of sour patches for my niece. Her favorite candy.

"Come on, Mom didn't spend money on them braces for nothing." I can see the frown on her face in my peripheral vision, which won't have an affect on me this time.

"She did waste her money, I only had them in for like a year." I say, shaking my head, I remember that day when the dentist told my mom that braces weren't necessary and a simple retainer would do, but of course, she didn't want that. "I don't want you taking it out every time you got to eat. I don't like that and you don't even wash your hands all the time." My mama said to me with a scrunched up face after the dentist said the word retainer. I can still see the sly smirk on his face, the way he fought the urge to laugh at my mother's perfect attempt to embarrass me.

"You know how Mom feels about crooked teeth. It's the equivalent of me hating to see you frown."

I turn my body toward the direction of the small stuffed animals, hoping to find something small and pink for Star. Every year, my sister and niece plan a special Valentine's Day celebration and Star makes me the cutest Valentine's Day cards and homemade art projects, like a bracelet or a necklace. In exchange, I get her her favorite candy and a pink stuffed animal.

Kassiah walks into my line of sight one more time, I roll my eyes and give her the faintest smile.

"There, happy now?" I grab a small, cute unicorn for Star and turn to Kassiah.

She rolls her eyes at me and grabs the cart, pushes past me, and snatches the small pink unicorn from me before throwing it in the cart.

"I was thinking about getting the unicorn but there was a pink rabbit." I call out from behind her.

"I don't want to be standing in the Holiday aisle forever before you realize you want the unicorn, besides rabbits symbolize sex and I don't want that for my child. She's 6." Kassiah continues to push the cart fast down the aisle, trying to beat the slow walkers who are walking in the same direction toward self-checkout.

"It's an animal." I lightly jog behind her, "Are you going to slow down? I thought you wanted to grab paper towels."

Kassiah comes to a stop at the self-checkout line. I stop beside her and try to catch my breath. Maybe I should start using the treadmill a little longer in the gym.

"I can get paper towels later, I want to make sure that we get you a new outfit for your date tonight." Kassiah's eyebrows dance across her forehead.

I groan. "For the love of God, Kassiah. I told you this is not a date."

Kassiah's facial features straighten out as her weight shifts to one side. "Sure, your super hot best friend with money always takes you out for dinner once a month and you don't think that it's because he likes you."

I roll my eyes. Of course Kassiah would call the man hot, I mean anybody would really, but there is a reason we are best friends and if all else fails, we agreed to get married if we didn't find someone by the age of twenty-eight. And the way things are going with him, I'm pretty sure I'll be the best man at his wedding.

"He's always busy with work, so we catch up." I shrug.

My best friend, Rosen, works for a prestigious accounting firm that travels to meet with their wealthy clients, so he is always busy. Unlike me, who just works in the bookstore my grandmother passed down to me (being I was the only one who likes books) and runs a successful vlog about book reviews and new releases. Sure, I missed the days when he and I would stay up late on the phone and watch our favorite show together, when we would pull all-nighters to listen to our favorite artist when they dropped a new album and learn the lyrics to our favorite songs. But now that things are super adulty between us, we settle for just a once a month thing. It's better than texting him all my issues throughout the week.

"Whatever, let's just find you something cute so he can drool all over you during dinner tonight."

I roll my eyes. Everytime Rosen takes me out, it's to some place he and his clients went to during one of their meetings. I had no idea there were this many restaurants in town, but then again, I don't know any outside of Apple Bee's and OutBack. Rosen's always claiming I'll love the crab cakes at each spot he takes me to. It's the only reason I allow him to drag me to those fancy restaurants.

After spending what felt like hours waiting in the dreaded line, Kassiah and I scanned our items and threw our bags in the back seat of her car before heading over to the new boutique that opened up a month ago in the Brookhaven shopping center. It's full of fast fashion but it makes my cheap ass look like I spent some type of money on myself. I ran out of all the dresses I saved for special occasions and I don't need someone pointing out that I wore the same dress twice.

As we walk through Sandra's clothing store, the smell of new clothing wafts through the air and soft R&B plays on the speaker. A store clerk with long boho braids smiles at me as she hangs new clothes on the rack. I immediately walk to the left side of the store, where new evening gowns hang in between the work attire and the party dresses.

My gaze automatically locks with a black dress that shimmers slightly in the light. I turn my back to see Kassiah looking at heels she has no business wearing in front of the window.

"Kassiah, come here." I aggressively whisper to her.

She shoots me a look, I watch as her eyes wander from me to the dress, a look of approval forming across her face.

"I like that, It'll make all your features pop." She says to me with a happy smile.

"You don't think I'll look like a halloween spokesperson with this?" I say, touching my natural ginger hair. I usually avoid wearing black to avoid people asking me if Halloween is my favorite holiday. Which it isn't, by the way, it's Christmas. I usually go for more browns and tans but it's something about this dress that catches my eye. It must be the sequins.

"I think nobody is going to ask you that when they see you in this." She says with a big smile.

I shrink under her megawatt smile and look up at the dress. I just hope Rosen is taking me somewhere that makes this dress appropriate.

Kassiah looks toward one of the available store clerks. "Excuse me, ma'am, Can you help us get this dress down? We'll need this in a medium size."

***

I tap my foot nervously in my cozy home, also left to me by my grandmother, who owned about 3 houses in the area after she divorced my grandfather. She left one to me and one to my sister. The third one, my family and I rent out and split the profit, which is great for my pockets. I look in the mirror and fluff out my hair, convincing myself that the ginger of my hair and the black of my dress do not remind me of Halloween, though the combination is always burned into my subconscious.

I pull out my phone and text my sister, Kassiah, second guessing my dress choice at the store. Maybe I should've spent more than twenty dollars.

Kassiah, I think the dress is too much.

What if he takes me to burger king this time.

Why would he take you to burger king?

Don't let your man sike you out

He's not my man

If you say so

The doorbell rings just as I was about to give my long winded speech of why I would never date my best friend. We made a pact in high school not to cross boundaries after that accidental kiss we shared after ninth grade winter formal.

**"Don't worry it won't happen again, It was just the vibes of the dance."**

**"Agreed."**

The doorbell rings again, making me jump out of my thoughts and walk gingerly in my heels to open the door. My feet hurt already, but at least I won't be too short compared to him. I open the door to see Rosen in a full on suit, black with a blue tie. His hair is cut and his beard is freshly trimmed, as if he just got out of the barbershop before coming over.

"You look amazing, Kay." Rosen says, slightly out of breath.

I look up to see a glimmer in his eye, he scans my face before turning away to cough and straightening his back.

"And I was worried I was over dressed." I smooth out a slight wrinkle in his suit. He smiles and captures my hand before it falls to my side, his thumb caressing the back of my hand, while the scent of sandalwood fills my nostrils. The cool February air greets me as we step outside to head to the car, the sun is almost completely gone under the pink clouds.

"Trust me, if the dress code switches up, I will let you know." He looks down at me with a small smile among his lips.

I nod, "Good, because if I put this on for you to take me to Mcdonalds, that would be embarrassing."

A hearty laugh comes out of Rosen. "That dress is too good for a McChicken."

I smile as Rosen opens the door for me. I sit in the passenger seat and watch Rosen jog to the driver's side before hopping in. I rest my elbow on the console between us and rest my chin in my hands.

"Will I like the crab cakes?" I smile.

He smirks. "I want you to be the judge of that."

***

### *Rosen*

Valet takes my keys as I pull into the parking lot. I tip the man a few bills before handing over my keys. I can't see Kayani's face through the tinted windows of my car but I can tell she's impressed, she always is.

I open the car door for her as a sense of awe spreads across her face. I smirk at the surprise in her eyes as she smooths the front of her dress before taking my hand. The restaurant is surrounded by a beautiful garden and the walls are almost all glass, like eating in a greenhouse. The greenery surrounding us glows by the fairy lights, illuminating the ground and the archways of the garden. I remember coming here a few weeks ago with a client as we talked about budgeting their expenses for retirement and all that boring jazz. I couldn't help but think what this place would look like at night. Especially here with Kayani.

"This place looks unreal." She scoffs with no look of disgust anywhere plastered on her soft features. The dress she wears is breathtaking, hugging the curves of her body and accentuates her hips and waist, making her even more curvier than I remember. My hand flinches to touch her and hold her close to me, to smell her signature vanilla scent, hoping that it will linger into my suit jacket and last throughout dinner and-

"What?" Kayani asks, looking at me with skepticism. I was staring a little too long. I'm always staring too long.

"Nothing" I look away and grab her hand. I catch my reflection in one of the windows and straighten my shoulders. I had just got my haircut for this dinner, a low fade, and made sure my hairline was straight as my spine. I picked out the nicest suit I could find and put on my favorite blue tie, which Kayani's mom gave to me when I graduated college. I smoothed out one side of my beard with my free hand and walked Kayani toward the front of the restaurant where reservations were waiting for us.

I sneak one more peek at Kayani, whose shoulders tense up the more we walk to the front. I can barely tell if she's breathing. I laugh on the inside before pulling her closer to me and wrap my arm around her shoulder, feeling the tension slowly release.

"Did I mention you look good? I almost fainted when you opened the door."

She cackles "You're the one that looks good, Mr. Gold chain and watch." She looks up at me with a beam of a smile on her face.

"I can get you one as well." I say as we wait for the couple in front of us to be seated.

"You know I'm not into the fancy stuff, that's a you thing." She shakes her head and looks around the restaurant, taking in the smell of seared meat and wine.

"I come from humble beginnings, I'm not so fancy." I let go of her and turn to face her, and she gives me a look as if I said a bunch of bull.

"What do you call this?" She motions to the restaurant and her outfit with a smug look on her face.

"I remember the nights where we talked about doing this together. I wanted to make that come true."

Her face softens before she takes my hand again, I walk to the front of the restaurant and am greeted by a lanky man with blond hair.

"Do you have a reservation with us?" He asks, clicking through some tabs on his computer.

"Yes, under Johnson. First name Rosen." I say, running my thumb over Kayani's hand.

"Ahh yes, I see." The host says to me after clicking a few buttons on his keyboard. "Are you here for our Valentine's night? Free bottle of wine to celebrate your love and a chef recommended steak dinner with Creme Brulee for dessert." He says so fast as he grabs our menus.

I open my mouth to speak but Kayani answers quickly

"Um absolutely not. We're just here to eat." She shifts her weight to her left leg before letting go of my hand to cross her arms over her chest.

The man looks taken aback before looking at me before giving a quick nod. "Um, yes right this way."

"Thanks." Kayani says bitterly before following the man to our table, gingerly walking in her heels.

I would swoop her off her feet right now and carry her to the table, but I don't want to make a scene – not after the one Kayani just made. I walk over to hold out her chair but she stops me and does it herself. I awkwardly sit across from her as the menus are laid out in front of us. I make no effort to listen to the man talk to us about wine specials and the server who will be with us. I just stare intently at the frown across Kayani's face

"What's wrong?" I question as the host walks away.

"Nothing, these heels just make my feet hurt." She says, rubbing her temples a little before placing her hand on her lap.

"Really? That's all." I ask.

She nods just as our server comes to take our orders.

"Hi. I'm Lindel, I'll be your server tonight. May I start you off with something to drink?"

"Red wine, doesn't matter the bottle, I trust your judgment." I shrug.

"White." Kayani snaps. Making us both look in her direction.

"Uh, can we have white wine instead. I don't really like red wine."

The waiter looks at me waiting for an approval. "You heard the lady."

He nods. "I'll be back with your wine."

Kayani sighs out in relief before sitting back in her chair. I lean forward and grab her calf; Her skin feels soft against my rough hands. She jumps but doesn't remove her leg from my hands. I remove her heel and gently rub her foot. Kayani leans back, relaxed in her chair. I chuckle and stare down at the menu.

"I don't need you being cranky because of these heels." I say, my voice a little bit raspier than usual.

"Sorry." Her cheeks darken along with the dimming lights. I look up to see a chandelier above us. "That's a nice light."

She nods. Not listening to my words, only feeling the magic of my hands against her foot.

"Tell me about work." I ask before grabbing her other leg and removing her heel to massage her foot.

"Well, the bookstore is doing great. I signed up to be a bookish influencer for a book box subscription company, fingers crossed I get it because they have the best skincare products in their boxes."

I chuckle. 'You use those products daily?"

Her eyes bulge in their sockets "Do I? I look forward to my skin care and reading nightly."

I smile "What else you got up your sleeve?"

She sits there in a trance thinking as my thumbs dig into the base of her foot. She lights up and looks at me with a megawatt smile. "I'll be getting some special editions in my bookstore. I partnered with a company."

"Really? You got any new ones to show me?"

"Do I?" She smiles.

Our waiter comes back with our wine, and of course, Kayani and I order the crab cakes and whatever sides come with it. Kayani sits barefoot, her feet resting in my lap as we sip our wine and talk about work. Kayani tells me about the bunch of reviews she made, books she read this month, and about her bookstore. And of course, I tell her about my travels and the clients I met. I tell her about the lunch I had with the client at this restaurant and how he raved about the food. It was okay at best, but he said dinner was always better.

"Rosen, this food better be good." She stares daggers at me. I quiet her down as our plates come out, crab cakes with mashed potatoes and asparagus.

She pulls out her phone and takes a picture of her food and me before she settles down to take a bite. "Try on the count of 3?" I ask, taking a fork full of crab cake.

She nods and takes a fork full of crab cake "1...2...3."

We simultaneously put our forks in our mouths, instantly, I taste the bland crab cake with nothing but filling of mostly breadcrumbs. Kayani looks at me and we both laugh, catching the eyes of a few people nearby. I spit my crab cake out in a napkin.

I watch as Kayani scrunches her face up to the mashed potatoes she put in her mouth.

"Chef must be tired from the full house."

I chuckle. "I'm sorry." I say, feeling bad she got dressed up to look so beautiful only to end up starving because of the food.

"You know, I kind of can go for Tacos." She says with a shrug.

"How about we get out of these clothes, get tacos and watch our show?" I ask with a tiny plea, anything to make up for this horrific food.

I watch as Kayani makes a face as a woman receives red roses right next to us.

"That sounds great right now." She says, avoiding eye contact with the whole world as she puts on her heels for us to leave.

# Chapter 2



*Kayani*

I opted out of my elegantly sexy dress for my baggy sweatpants, which have seen better days, and my black tank top with a hole in the trim, right in the middle of my breast. We decided to order our tacos for delivery instead of picking them up. I didn't feel like going to any more places today and Rosen could sense that due to the face I made when he asked if we were picking them up. Rosen sent me the money for the tacos and I ordered our usual. Two orders of chicken birria tacos, one order of birria tacos (for us to share), and two large watermelon guava agua frescas. My stomach rumbles just thinking about them.

I grab my comfy blanket and my current romance book before heading down the stairs where Rosen waits for me. I let him borrow the clothes that I stole from him back in our college days. He wears gray sweatpants and an oversized marvel shirt that I remember taking when he went to see the movie without me when it first came out.

"All comfortable?" I ask as I sit on the couch and lay my blanket over my lower body. Rosen moves closer to me and grabs the remote from in between the tiny space between us.

"You've been watching our show without me?" He asks as he goes to the pre-recorded shows that fill up my DVR

"No, I haven't been, but there is this new show I've been trying to get you to tune into forever." I snatch the remote from him and turn on my most frequented streaming service, choosing one of the animes I spent last Saturday watching until I fell asleep with a slice of pizza in my hand.

"How many episodes have you watched?" He questions as he places his arm along the back of the chair.

"I think maybe about three episodes" I say, cracking open my romance book.

"You want me to turn on the light?" He asks me as I squint to see the words illuminated by the TV.

"No, It's fine. You watch the show. I need to finish the last couple pages of this book."

I can feel Rosen's eyes burn a hole in the side of my face as I begin to read. I shift under his gaze, trying to focus on the scene in front of me and not the glare Rosen is giving me right about now. I look at him through the corner of my eye, seeing him now fixated on the TV. The light from the TV illuminates his features, he almost looks fake, like those AI pictures everyone has been making on my instagram feed these days. His glasses are also still on from when he was driving earlier and his beard is cut low and well groomed, making his jaw line pop. I avert my eyes and continue to read my book, finishing up the last chapter before the epilogue. My phone buzzes with a delivery notification and my stomach rumbles instantly.

Rosen laughs and pauses the TV before episode three plays on the television.

"Someone is hungry." He gets up from his seat and immediately it starts to feel a little chilly in here. I put my book down and smile when I see the food held up high in his hands.

I scoot off the chair and make my way to the floor as Rosen brings the food and drinks down before carefully sitting next to me. I take out our food as Rosen grabs the remote to turn the TV back on.

"So you like the show, huh?" I smirk as I grab my book, opening up to the page where I left off.

"Sure do." Rosen says to me before snatching my book and placing it under his leg. He smirks, unable to look at me. I know that if he did, he would burst into laughter. This man is so corny.

I frown, "Was that really necessary?" The light from the television danced across his face, making his brown skin look amazing under the blue rays.

"Highly, I was getting confused why you had me sit here in the dark to watch TV while you read. The silence was killing me." He leans back dramatically as the recap of last episode replays in the background. "I thought this was supposed to be a day for us." He fake pouts.

"There was the TV." I shrug before grabbing my birria taco.

"Yeah but your voice is the one I rather listen to. Not the little guy on the screen yelling about fighting formations."

I giggle before dipping my tacos in the consume, I can see the huge smile on Rosen's face in the corner of my eye. My heart flutters at the site. I force myself to look away as a feeling of confusion instills in me from my reaction.

Maybe my loneliness has me confused about my interaction with Rosen but this is something we always do. I don't see anything wrong with eating tacos on the floor with my best friend, forcing him to watch an anime that he said he'd never watch. Nothing about this is romantic.

"I ordered the tacos from a new spot." I say before dipping my taco again.

Rosen smirks before grabbing his birria taco. "So if this place is nasty then I can blame it on you."

"You're the reason we're in this situation in the first place." I laugh.

"Actually, my client is. He was the one that told me the food was good."

"You shouldn't have believed him." I giggle, shaking my head.

"Well, I liked his shirt." Rosen says, earning a playfully agitated look on his face. His smile creeps up slowly on his face.

"On the count of three?" He asks before dipping his tacos in the juices.

I nod and on the count of three, we both take a bite of our tacos, experiencing the most pleasurable cheese pull ever. The tacos were juicier than I expected and flavor erupted into my mouth; my eyes roll back as I chew slowly, leaning my back against the chair for support.

Rosen's laugh fills the room. "I was going to ask if you liked the tacos but I can see that you do."

"This might have to be my new taco spot." I say through a mouthful of birria.

Rosen is probably the only guy that I ever pigged out in front of. I blamed him for my curvy shape, always taking me out to restaurants and picking me up food in college and when he first started his job. I spent many early mornings in the gym because of that and earned myself a nice body that seems to be the only thing these men want from me and a healthy lifestyle that I can't seem to shake off.

"Don't eat there without me. We tried this place together."

I roll my eyes. "First, I can't watch Surviving without you, now I can't eat tacos."

"You can eat tacos, just not from this place." He chuckles.

I pout and slouch against the chair. "Whatever." I say, not putting up a fight. I like having sacred things with Rosen and if the taco spot is now one of them, count me in.

"Speaking of surviving. Can we catch up on our newest episodes? I stopped paying attention to this."

My eyes meet with his and that award winning smile of his comes rushing back. Should I be attracted to this? Of course, every girl is attracted to a smile, it's a nice one, especially Rosen's. I'm not attracted to the man attached to it.

I repeat that through my subconscious. Kassiah's words ring through my head. She swears there is something between us, she always has, but to me, it's nothing like that.

"Earth to Kayani." Rosen waves his hand in front of my face. A glob of meat falls into my consume, splashing a little bit on my leg.

"Yeah, we can watch it." I reach over and grab some napkins, dabbing off some of the juices before finishing the taco.

Rosen grabs the remote and turns to another streaming service where our show awaits us. I watch his jaw line pop as he chews slowly on the food in his mouth. Watching him makes me hungry. I snap out of the trance his jawline has me in and eat another taco.

The show loads up on the television, leaving Rosen and I in comfortable silence as we eat our food. A little circle loads on the left hand side of my screen, indicating commercials. I groan loudly when I see that same chocolate commercial to promote Valentine's Day play on my screen. The chocolate looks good, but the thought of eating it as a gift from someone on Valentine's Day makes me queasy.

I stare hard at my tacos. "Fuck Valentine's day." I whisper under my breath before taking a bite of my tacos.

***

### *Rosen*

Kayani is in that mood again. And it's not until I hear the soft whisper of fuck and Valentine's Day in the same sentence.

"You're not a lover as I thought you were." I say, watching her body slump in a state of agitation over her tacos. My comment awakens her, almost as if she's remembering I'm right here.

"What are you talking about?" She asks, clueless, though from the slight discoloration in her face, she was not expecting me to hear her.

"What's your beef with Valentine's Day?" Her reaction in the restaurant starts to make sense. Everything was fine until the host mentioned something about Valentine's Day specials. I never really cared much for Valentine's Day myself, but for Kayani, she seems to hate this holiday with every fiber of her being.

"No beef. It's just that day sucks." She shrugs, trying to be nonchalant but it's not fooling me.

"Has to be a reason why you hate it. Like, I don't like Halloween, because my mom never let me dress up as a superhero."

She laughs, remembering my tragic tale. My mom never let me dress up on my own but always wanted family costumes. Embarrassing things like dressing up as sunny side up eggs and the little workers from Charlie and the chocolate factory. I never cared for it after the 5th time she made me dress up and never celebrated it after I was old enough to decline dressing up.

"I'm sorry your mother did that to you." Laughter remains in her voice, which gets a little smile out of me.

"No need to be sorry. I need to know why you don't like Valentine's Day." I shrug.

Kayani groans loudly, she shifts her body toward me and looks down at the fuzzy carpet in front of her. "I just never had a good one."

I pause the show when I hear the theme song start and face my body toward her.

"Repeat that?"

She rolls her eyes and shakes her head. "Can you just play the show? This is stupid."

I reach for her hand, forcing her eyes to look into mine. "It's not dumb. It's bothering you so let it out. You heard my hate for Halloween plenty of times."

A faint smile spreads across her lips. "It's just, I never had a proper Valentine. Proper man at that, but I always get the runt of the litter."

I sit up straight, hearing the slight sadness in her voice. I nod slowly, urging her to go on.

"I've had just about every horrible date you can think of, I've had a guy who only wanted to receive gifts, not get me anything. I've been stood up, found out I was a side piece. Oh and get this. One guy forgot to give me something on Valentine's Day and ended up giving me half dead roses." She shakes her head, laughing a little, "I always get rotten roses on this day. Figuratively and literally."

I frown, hearing one of the best girls I know get treated like this is something that doesn't sit right with me. My hands ache to hold her, to go out and get her a rose for every time she's cried over one of those losers.

"Damn, why have you never told me about this?"She scoffs a little, "So you can get me flowers? Don't be silly."

Ouch. I bite the inside of my cheek, hearing the rejection come out smoothly from her mouth. "I mean, I could've done something to make the day less worse."

"But you always save the day." She smiles softly.

"I know. But what about old dude last year? He seemed to have you head over heels."

She lets out a long sigh, "I mean, last year my granddad passed away the day before Valentine's Day, and the guy I was dating blocked me in my sleep." She shakes her head at the thought. Envy runs through my veins, remembering how sweetly she sounded on the phone telling me about that guy. Along with the tears that flooded through my phone when she told me about him and how her grandfather had just passed.

I flew back home that same day, just to make sure she felt better. I had scheduled a piano lesson in the city I was in at the time. My parents were renewing their vows and I promised I'd play their song on the piano at their ceremony. I had gotten rusty over the years after not playing and doing something other than working in a new city every time was calling my name. But hearing the devastation on the phone made my own heart break. I took a flight at the same time as my lesson and rushed to her side. We ate her favorite ice cream that I hate. But I only did it for her. I can still feel her wet face on my shirt and see the hallmark movies she forced me to watch. I learned the song on youtube with Kayani as my audience.

"I remember." I nod. The details feel vivid in my mind almost like watching an out of body experience.

"Yeah. Valentine's Day is a day to show the one you love that you love them, right? Or care about them?" She questions herself. "I never had that." She shrugs. "And I'm fine with that."

"Not having a lover or Valentine's Day?" My brows furrow, waiting for her response.

"Both. I have my books and my books love me."

I shake my head. I've never experienced real love outside of witnessing it from my parents. I had girls who were interested in me and girls I was interested in. But none of the girls ever felt right to take things any further than a few dates.

"That's not love. You have to experience it in real life."

"My love life exists within the pages of a romance novel." She grabs her blanket and wraps it around her.

I think about my parents when those words escape her mouth. Their love can stand the end of time. And there is definitely something about them that can be written into a romance novel. I'd call it a best selling book if it was to be written. I guess that's why I'm still single. Looking for something just like that.

"Are you serious?" I smirk, her words feel concrete as if it's set in stone where her love life begins and ends.

She nods. "That's where it exists these days. There's always a happy ending there."

I frown feeling the solemn words. The pity party that Kayani has thrown for herself, confettied by dead rose petals

She grabs the remote from me and turns the show back on. "Now, watch the show." Her words are final as she crosses her arms over her chest.

I can't help but stare at her a little longer, I can still see her tears, feel the disappointment in her eyes when she sees no roses to match her beauty. No man should even think about treating a girl as beautiful as Kayani like that.

Before I know it the words escape my mouth. "Let me be your Valentine."

Kayani pauses the TV instantly, looking at me as if I grew two heads. "Excuse me." Confusion screams across her face. Her eyes scan my face rapidly, hoping to search for the answer.

I form my fingers into a heart, hoping that it will suffice in the replacement of flowers. "Will you be my Valentine?"

Her lips partly open but I rush to cut her off.

"Hear me out." My heart pounds as I speak the words that burst through my mind like an open dam. Explaining myself before she leaves me with an answer I refuse to hear.

I tap my phone, seeing the date February 7th before continuing.

"There's seven days left until Valentine's day. Let me show you how a real Valentine's Day is supposed to be every day until then."

"Why seven days?" Her head tilts to the side, a look of confusion still engraved on her face

"To make up for all your bad ones and then some." I feel out of breath as If I ran a whole marathon. My heart pounds in my ears, making it hard to hear her breathing.

"And this is because you care about me?" She questions.

"Yes." I nod.

"As a friend?" Her eyebrows raise

The words sting me but I nod my head yes anyway. "Let me raise your standards." I can hear the blood flow from my pounding heart as I wait painfully for her answer.

She smiles, which gives me all the confidence I need.

"Watch the show, please." She says, pressing play on the television.

I scoot closer to her and put my arm around her shoulder. I stare down at Kayani, unable to focus on the show, only on how I will make her feel special.

# Chapter 3

*Kayani*

If it wasn't for my love of fitness and books, I would be sleeping well past 5 am on a Sunday, but my life wouldn't be right if I didn't keep my routine. After scrubbing my face to look a little less crusty and throwing on my gym clothes, which are just high waisted purple leggings and a baggy white t-shirt that matches my sports bra underneath. I find myself staring out the window in my kitchen, dreading my early mornings.

I grab myself a banana and my creatine before stuffing it in my gym bag. I hold my warm mug of hot water with lemon juice and Cayenne pepper that I have been drinking to help with my excessive bloating and feel the cool gentle air from the window.

The cold air will wake me up as soon as I step outside to warm up my car. I chug the warmish drink, making a face when the heat from the pepper and drink burn the back of my throat. I stumble to my front door, smacking my right cheek to wake me. "Come on Ani, can't fall asleep behind the wheel."

The cold air greets me as I swing open the front door. I walk out into the frigid air, seeing a familiar car parked in front of my car.

The window rolls down slowly and Rosen's smiling face greets me on the other side.

"Cold?" He questions, a small smirk on his lips.

A severe shiver runs down my body, jolting my body, making Rosen laugh. I take a few more steps to the car, feeling my hamstrings tighten from the cold and gladly take my place in the passenger seat of Rosen's car.

"What are you doing here this morning?"

The warmth from Rosen's car feels amazing on my skin. I put my hands against the vents, warming up my frigid hands.

"I know you like to go to the gym in the mornings, so I thought I'd join you. Would be better than working out alone later anyway." He shrugs, but I can see the remnants of a smile threatening to break.

"I feel like you're up to something." I squint my eyes at him, trying to figure out what's up his sleeve.

"I could be. Or maybe I just wanted to work out with my best friend." His smile is so suspicious but annoyingly cute.

"Is this because of the whole Valentine debacle?" I question, seeing the sudden discoloration on Rosen's face. I had a hard time sleeping last night, thinking about Rosen's Valentine proposal. Did I reveal too much about my personal self and now he feels so much pity for me?

I always feel as if I vent too much to him but it's hard for me not to. He makes me a motor mouth when I am around him. I just don't want him to think he has to save the day for me all the time. I internalize or vent to Kassiah, which saves me from the pity act because she gives it to me like it is. Something she got from my mother.

But I couldn't help but overthink this last night, which is one of the reasons I was tossing and turning all night and not the fact that I was wrapped up in hot blankets with the heat blasting.

"Listen, I promised myself that I would show you a real Valentine's, so I'm making up for that. Think about your first bad Valentine's Day experience."

I sit back in my seat and think about the time in highschool, my junior year when this guy who I was talking to made a whole Valentine's Day proposal for another girl and made me record it. Rosen kept asking me if I was okay on the way home and gave me a Valentine's Day card he made for me in art class.

"Okay." I say once the image has been made clear to me.

"Now, replace that memory with the ones I'm going to make with you today."

Rosen turns off the light in his car and puts his car into drive before heading off to the gym. We listen to my favorite songs on the way there. And I mean every single one of the songs that played through the speaker was a song I adored. Rosen might be better at this than I thought.

As we pull up to an almost empty parking lot, we find a spot closest to the gym doors so that we can make a quick break for it.

"Put this on so you can be extra warm." Rosen reaches back and pulls out a light gray hoodie with fur on the inside that reminds me almost of a blanket hoodie.

"Have I ever told you how much of a life saver you are?" I bat my eyelashes and pretend to be very infatuated with him.

This earns me a hearty laugh from him. He mushes my head and points to the pockets. "Take the gloves out for your hands." He reaches over and grabs my bag from in front of me before getting out of the car. A small amount of cold air blasts through the car as he exits with his bag and mine. He walks over to my side and opens the door with both of our bags hanging on both shoulders.

"Thank you, Rosen, really." I take his hand as I get out of the car.

He shrugs nonchalantly "I'm just being your hero." he winks

I roll my eyes. Maybe I shouldn't have made the joke after all.

He laughs and jogs to the front of the building to evade the cold and I'm two steps behind him. I wonder if this will count for my cardio for the day.

Rosen opens the door for me as I enter the building, it's warm and empty just how I like it. The gym is charming. I've been a member since it opened three years ago. The gym is a teal color with all black equipment.

I walk to the corner where I usually drop my stuff and immediately begin to warm up. Rosen drops my bags against the wall and joins me for my warm up.

"What are we hitting today, boss?" He mimics my warm up to a tea, which warms me up on the inside.

"Today is a glute day." I finish the last of my warm ups and head over to my bag where I prepare to make my creatine.

"You prepared to be sore today?" He smirks.

"I'm good at leg day as you can see." I say motion to my body. His eyes travel down my body with a sly smile on his face.

"You're right about that. I'm still going to push you, though."

I turn quickly, fighting the urge to fan myself from the look Rosen just gave me. I walk over to the weights and put them on the bar for my squat.

Rosen walks up behind me. "You need my help?"

I look up into the mirror in front of me making eye contact through the glass. "I think I'm good." I say, making him step back a little bit.

I get into form before taking the bar off the plate and doing a squat easily. Rosen frowns, shaking his head before putting the bar back on the rack.

"What?" I ask, confused.

"You hit that too easy, add more weight."

I laugh "It's the creatine."

He shakes his head once more. "Creatine my ass. Add weight."

I give Rosen a once over, giving him a stare down which he doesn't budge from. I huff before walking to add more weight. I'll show him for sure that it's the creatine.

I get in squatting position and lift the bar off. I stumble a little, the extra weight throwing me off.

"Let me help." Rosen says, he stands right behind me, his hands almost grazing mine as he places his open palm right under my fist. I can smell the old spice deodorant he threw on. His body heat waves off of him, making me even hotter.

"Whenever you're ready." He speaks gently to me.

I close my eyes before slowly squatting with Rosen mimicking my movements. I feel as if I'm sitting on his lap, His lower body grazes mine as I lift up. I look at him through the mirror, his face is almost buried in my big ginger fro. My heart pounds at his proximity.

"Again." He says, I watch his eyes roam to my backside through the glass before he makes eye contact with me again. He gently bites his lip before walking up closer to me to spot me for my next squat.

I swallow the lump in my throat and take a deep breath before hitting the squat with Rosen in close proximity. If the next six days are anything like this. I don't know how I'll defend myself to Kassiah.

***

### *Rosen*

No amount of water could erase the flustered feeling I got after working out with Kayani. The blistering cold was nothing to me after feeling the heat from her body earlier. I caught myself smiling at work on more than one occasion and all I did was spot the girl doing squats. A little too closely, but it was worth it, smelling her signature sugary vanilla scent.

I put on my watch and fix the color on my brown plaid flannel shirt before spraying my cologne. Today is the love fest, a yearly event on the other side of town, usually. I've been once or twice with a girl back in high school but this year, I want to take Kayani. Ease into the dates and romance I have planned for her this week and what better way to start than at a fair date.

Before walking out of the door, I grab the roses I picked up for her after work. A perfect hue in the middle of pink and red and not a dead leaf in sight. I put the roses in the passenger seat and buckle in the flowers to make sure they are safe from the trip.

My knuckles turn a shade lighter from my grip on the wheel. I take in a deep breath, trying to fight the nerves for my night with Kayani. Though I hang out with her all the time, this feels different than showing her a few good dates, but showing her that I can be the one for her. I've been fighting my feelings for Kayani since that winter dance kiss. I planned to admit my feelings for her that night but when she came to me expressing the mistake, I knew I had to fight my feelings and make sure that we stayed friends. I couldn't lose her over that.

When I get to the house, Kayani stands under the street light in front of her house looking casual, but to me she looks amazing. She wears a cropped black puffer jacket with fur interior and tight denim jeans with black knee high boots. Her natural ginger hair is slicked up into a high puff and black mittens cover her ears.

I pull the car up in front of her, making sure the heat is blasting before getting out of the car to open the passenger side door for her. She looks up at me with a smug smile. "If you're not wearing a coat, that means the place we're going to is inside?"

I chuckle. "You know I keep a coat in the backseat of my car in the winter."

She giggles before it comes to an abrupt stop followed by a shocking gasp. "Rosen." She says before unbuckling the seat belt to grab the flowers. She stares lovingly at the roses and my heart smiles at the small victory I've accomplished. I jog to the other side and get into the car and pull my phone out, taking off guard pictures of Kayani as she smells the roses.

"Life is good when you smell the roses, huh." I chuckle.

She gives me a radiant smile before looking at me. "Thank you, Rosen, I really don't know what to say." Her voice, clearly in awe just by the small gesture of roses. It makes me smile but breaks my heart, knowing that no man has ever done anything as simple as this for her.

I reach over and put my hand on her knee. "If you think this is the best place. Just wait until we get to our destination."

***

Love Fest is just as the name describes. Pink and red lights expand over the field, illuminating the field in a surreal glow. Rides are decorated with pink streamers and stuffed bears to give the mood and rose petals quite literally sprinkle the ground. Game booths are showing off big stuffed animals and stuffed hearts for you to win your lover, and kissing booths stand on each side of the games. That must be for lonely people. People sell roses and mini boxes of chocolates, while a giant cartoonish designed heart walks around for people to take pictures. The gentle breeze wafts the smell of sweets through the air. Mostly everything is deep fried or covered in chocolate. Most people love both of those things.

I hold Kayani close to me as we walk through the crowds of couples and families who took their kids out to enjoy the festivities. The fest lasts all week until Valentine's Day, where they have a big show with colored smoke and dancers. My mom went to the show last year, which inspired her to take ribbon dancing classes every thursday.

"You know, I've never been to Love Fest. I always wanted to go but then I hated Valentine's Day and the colors pink and red."

"But you always hated the color red." I chuckle.

She smiles shyly and puts her hands in her pockets. "You're right about that but now I really hate it."

"Well, now that we're here. What do you think of it?"

She pauses and looks up at a floating cupid above us before answering.

"Like Cupid himself threw this place together."

"You never cared much for Valentine's Day, have you?"

"I guess you can say that." I shrug.

"Well, hopefully, I'm changing your mind." I raise my eyebrows with a hint of a smile on my face.

"It takes more than flowers and cheesy carnival rides to make me change my mind." Her face is flushed from the cold weather. Maybe I should've taken her on a date indoors.

I grab her cold hands into mine "I know, let me show you." I lead her to a concession stand and buy us chocolate covered strawberries and hot chocolate, which they decorated with whip cream and pink & red sprinkles.

"Even the beverages are romantified." She giggles and takes a sip of her warm hot chocolate.

"Does this help the cold?" I ask, taking a sip of mine. I can tell they used water instead of milk.

"A little. But you know what would help even more?"

"What?"

She points to a giant white bear holding a heart. "If you won that bear for me."

I look at the game associated with it. Basketball, one of the things that I love. I used to play in high school but quit when I got to college. NBA was never in my dreams, but I always played for fun.

"Let's see if you're still in your prime." She says with a smirk.

I take another sip of my hot chocolate and place the chocolate covered fruits on top so that it doesn't get cold. "You're on." I say, accepting the challenge.

I walk up the empty station and give the man five dollars to play. "If you make every shot within the 30 seconds you can win a big bear. Or you can settle for one of the other prizes if you lose, miss more than three, win nothing at all."

"You better win that bear." Kayani screams at me through the howling wind.

I chuckle and grab one of the balls off the cart. I picture myself standing on the court with my dad. Him telling me the perfect way to shoot the ball, making me practice every time until I never missed. I was a dangerous man at the free throw line in high school because of this.

The timer begins and I start to make my shots, watching the balls go in the hoop instantly. I would take a second to rest before reshooting. Taking longer if the ball didn't feel right in my hands.

"Look at you," Kayani cheers.

With one ball left, I feel my heart pounding in my chest. I almost want to shoot it with my eyes closed. I reset, watching the clock hit five seconds before shooting the last ball once the breeze calmed.

The man looks at me impressed when the last ball makes it in. Kayani cheers and raises herself on her tippy toes in a little jump, careful not to spill the drink.

"What can I get you?" The man in the station asks as he grabs his stick to get the bears down.

"That white one."

He hands me the bear before picking up the others. I walk to Kayani who looks as if she is ready to throw the drinks down and hug the bear. She drinks the last of her hot chocolate before handing me mine. I down mine, which is now cold thanks to the wind. And take a bite of a strawberry while Kayani hugs the bear.

"Thank you, thank you, thank you." She squeals like a schoolgirl. Rocking the bear as if it was her niece.

"You're giving that bear more love than me." I say, popping another chocolate covered fruit in my mouth.

She steps forward, closing the space between us as she looks up into my eyes.

"Thank you, Rosen." She grabs a chocolate covered strawberry from my hand and takes a bite, still looking me in the eyes. Her lips pucker from the juices of the berry as she chews, Suddenly, I wish I was that berry.

I open my mouth to say something but can't think with the way she stares at me. I want to ask her if she feels the same, if she's wondering how beautiful I think she is under the soft glow of the pink fluorescents.

The space between us feels closer as I feel my body pressing against the huge white stuffed animal blocking us from connecting.

Kayani looks up suddenly with a huge smile on her face. "It's snowing," she says.

I look around us, seeing the little snow flurries around us. Kayani shivers a little bit under the sudden breeze. I go to unzip my coat before she stops me.

"Let's just go somewhere warm." She says, stopping me from my heroic nature.

I grab her hand as she cuddles her giant bear for warmth. We walk outside of the festival area and down the street to where some of the businesses are. Some open later in hopes that the love fest drives some business.

"Rosen, look, a bookstore." Kayani gasps, seeing the sign "Juniper Books" in big bold letters. She grabs my hand, dragging me to the store, and I can do nothing but laugh.

We walk inside the store when we see the open sign still flipped. The bookstore is cozy, with lavender walls and cream rugs and decor. Most of the books I see are romance, and I watch as Kayani walks around the store, exploring the books on the shelves. I take out my phone to record the moment. Watching as she explores her peace.

"Rosen, this whole store is a vibe. Come here" She says, pulling a book off the shelf. The book has a shirtless man on the front. I frown looking at it.

She giggles at my reaction before grabbing another with a similar cover. "Relax, my followers say I should get into more urban romances and this was one of the ones they recommended."

I frown. "They couldn't recommend you one with a cute cover or something. Like the ones you read."

Kayani bursts into laughter at my words, confusing me. "Did I say something wrong?"

She just continues to laugh as she moves slowly down the aisle for more books.

"Would you read Romance?" She asks me before grabbing another book. She eyes me curiously when I gain her attention.

"I may try it out if something catches my attention."

She nods and grabs my hand, leading me to the front of the store where books line a rack in brown paper.

"Pick a book based on the small details."

"But I can't see the cover and blurb." I say, looking at the few words written on the paper.

"Good, because you judge a book by its cover." Kayani says, picking up one of the wrapped books. "You start reading, I can finally have a reading friend. Kassiah doesn't want to read with me." She frowns.

I chuckle and grab a book, the same one that I've been staring at with the words childhood friends to lovers written at the top.

"Is that the one?" She asks me before moving to the check out.

I nod and grab the books from her to pay for them. "Yeah, I want to know what you mean when you say your love life exists inside of them."

She smiles, looking over my arm as the lady rings up the books. "You should sorta kind of feel it in this moment." She says, waiting for me to pay before taking the bag from me, leaving me with my single book as she motions for me to follow her back to the car.

# Chapter 4

*Rosen*

I couldn't wait to see Kayani again, not after with her words running through my mind. After taking her back home. I wrote a list of things I want Kayani to experience in a relationship. A relationship with me that is, and since I stayed late yesterday, I called off work today and joined my parents for breakfast.

My mom always cooks breakfast in the morning and I couldn't remember a time when she hadn't, even when she was angry or mad at him. I would always wake up to the smell of turkey bacon and when she was feeling really nice, she made french toast, which was his favorite and mine, too.

"You taking a day off is very rare." My mom says as she puts a plate in front of me.

"And coming to spend it with us is even rarer." My dad looks at me with scrunched up eyebrows, confusion well spread on his face.

"I had a great time last night. I didn't want to risk doing a bad job because I woke up tired."

My dad looks at me horrified. "Rosen, your mother is right there." My dad gives me a warning look.

"Get your mind out the gutter, dad. I'm trying to say I went on a date last night." I shrug. Still unable to get her words out of my mind.

My mother leans forward, intrigued with this new bit of information. "Really? May I ask who is the lucky girl?"

I take a fork full of eggs into my mouth and chew them slowly before I give out this most recent information.

"Well, I took Kayani to Love Fest last night. Then we hit up a bookstore." The evidence of snow had disappeared, the slightly warmer temperature and sunny sky had made the soft flakes disappear by the time I pulled into my parents driveway.

"It's about time you guys go together." My mom squeals with excitement. She frowns as if disappointed that I waited too long. I can see the words 'I want grandkids' written across her forehead.

"And she actually let you take her out on a date? What happened to the pact?"

My mom snaps her head towards me. "Yeah, what about the pact?"

I let out a sigh, knowing that I will have a lot of explaining to do. "The other night, Kayani was telling me about all her horrible Valentine's dates. So, this week, I wanted to make up for all her bad times."

These words earn a wide grin from my dad. "That a boy. Make her realize she's always had her Valentine."

"I want my grandkids," My mom takes a fork full of eggs and stares at me as if I can give her the news we're expecting at this very moment.

"Dionne." My dad shoots my mom a glare, begging her to stop. I can feel the second hand embarrassment from my dad from here.

I snort, trying not to choke on a piece of bacon I'm chewing on. "Mom, don't worry about me." I still feel her gaze on me, though the silence around us is awkward.

"I'll take your word for it." She says before turning her attention back to her breakfast plate.

I make eye contact with my dad, who nonverbally tells me to ignore her as we eat the rest of our breakfast in silence.

After spending time with my parents, I walk through the downtown area, decorated to fit the love fest theme on the other side of town. Down here is where you find most of your small shops and diners. When Kayani and I were little, we would always visit the corner store down the street from my parents and get peppermint bark chocolate, which was Kayani's favorite. There was also a little diner right next door where we would meet up after school before my basketball games to share a plate of fries. That was always our weekly splurge. They added a mall down the road, which surprisingly has done good for this area. People always come here when they can't find what they need in the mall. However, the mall is my destination and I know exactly what I need is there.

I walk into the abandoned mall, it's midday on a weekday and the usual suspects who crowd this place are at work or at school, which makes getting out of here a whole lot quicker. I walk through the empty mall, hearing the varieties of music playing through the small shops and the smells of food and perfume waft through the air.

The image of Kayani's face lighting up when I gave her that bear yesterday is engraved in my mind, so much so that it brings me to my destination. Build-A-Bear. I always want to see her face light up over the small things, the big things. I'll always live for that moment, to see her eyes sparkle at the love she deserves. Because no woman should have to suffer through years of mistreatment and feel undeserving.

I walk straight into the store, looking for the perfect bear for her until landing on the Valentine's Day Bear. Since it's Kayani's first real Valentine's Day, I have to commemorate the moment with something heartfelt like this. The store blasts music that I only really hear on the ads on television. The same songs I heard when I was growing up as a kid.

My mom took me here once and it was actually for Kayani's older sister Kassiah's birthday party.

"Hi, Did you find your new friend today?" One of the women in the bright blue shirts asks me as she stares at the lifeless bear in my hands. I stare at the pink and red colors, the ones Kayani has told me she hates, hoping that this changes her mind.

"Yes." I couldn't help but smile as I handed the bear over to her.

"She must be a very special girl." The woman says, her hair is white and thin in a short updo. I can tell she's working again after being bored from retirement.

"She is, this is our first Valentine's together. I want to make it one she will always remember." I stuff my hands in my jean pocket, feeling a little weird to confess my heart to a stranger.

"It will be the first of many." She gives me a smile as best as she can before we walk over to the fill station where she showed me the colored hearts and recording devices. "Pick a heart for your furry friend, and if you want, you can record a message."

I smirk while picking up the recording device. My heart pounds as I think about the type of thing I should say to her. I take in a deep breath, confessing the words that I am too scared to say into the device and hand the device and heart to the worker.

Her lip pokes out in a pout as she puts her hand over her heart. "Aww. How firm would you like your bear?"

I chuckle. "Pretty firm. I think that this bear will be hugged on a lot once it's given."

She nods as she begins to stuff the bear. "Oh absolutely." Her agreement is a little inaudible as she steps on the pedal, filling the bear with fluff.

Before heading over to Kayani's bookstore, I pick her up some lunch and her favorite specialty coffee from the diner we love so much and a fresh bouquet of roses. Upon entering, the bell rings, signalling my arrival and the smell of books mixed with the distinct smell of lemon and Lavender air freshener that Kayani has been obsessed with filled the air.

I hold onto the flowers and food with dear life as I hear the soft and subtle footsteps of a person coming from the back. My shoulders tense when I see Kayani's older sister, Kassiah, coming from the back, followed by her niece who frowns from discomfort.

"Hey, Star." I smile, avoiding the confused gaze Kassiah gives me. I bend down and drop the flowers and the drink tray on the ground to give Star a high five.

She gives me a weak one before speaking to me. "My stomach hurts."

"I'm sorry." I frown and rub my tummy as if mine were aching.

"Mommy gave me medicine. I'm just waiting to poop." She says, causing Kassiah to chuckle behind her. I look up over Star's head to see Kassiah still eyeing me with suspicion.

"Kassiah, who's at the front?" Kayani yells, my heart flutters and I immediately grab the items from off the floor and stand up on my feet. Waiting to see Kayani. She comes out from behind the bookcases, a cute little apron around her. She wears a green sweater dress and short fluffy boots.

The look I live for lights up her face when she sees the items in my hands.

"Rosen, what are you doing here? Shouldn't you be at work?" She asks as she checks the clock. She stops just in front of me. I almost can't move, I remind my muscles to work as I hand her the flowers.

"I had off today and wanted to surprise you." I say, handing Kayani the roses and food.

"You went to our fav?" She picks up the to-go cup holder with the bag on top and places it down before grabbing the coffee cup and sipping on her favorite. Her eyes roll back as she sips it and takes a small sip.

"This is so sweet, Rosen, thank you." She takes in the sweet smell of flowers, she glows when she exhales, a peace so beautiful surrounding her.

"That's not all." I say, handing her the big house shaped box with her new stuffed animal.

Kayani's eyes droop, seeing the box in my hand. "Rosen, this is–"

I cut her off, "I recorded something for you. Promise you won't listen until Valentine's day?"

She holds the box as if I placed a precious jewel in her hands. She nods slowly, a surreal smile on her face. "I promise."

Before I know it, Kayani's arms wrap around me and instantly it feels like a weight has been lifted off my shoulders. God, I love her.

Kassiah stares daggers into me as we untangle ourselves from each other. I shift uncomfortably before giving Kayani a side hug.

"I'm about to head out. I will text you plans for later." I say before saying my goodbyes to Kassiah and Star and heading out of the store, feeling as if I could walk on Air.

***

### *Kayani*

Kassiah just stares at me as I take a bite into my chicken sandwich that Rosen got for me. Star lays on one of the couches by the window on her tablet as shoppers enter my cozy bookstore. I smile at them, keeping my food behind my pearly whites so lettuce won't stick out to them.

I watch as they scan the bookstore, the light blue walls almost look white with the shining sun through the window. Books line the shelves on the wall, separated by different romance genres. I tried to read each and every book on my shelf, which would be impossible but I do spend most of my time reading. I love discovering new books for my store; one of my prides about my store is the amount of indie authors that line the shelves along with the traditionally published ones. It makes my heart happy seeing the amount of love that each book gets from being displayed.

"Hi, let us know if you need anything." Kassiah says for me as I slowly begin to chew my food again.

"Thank you." I say when the customers lose themselves in the shelves.

"Oh, no problem." Kassiah says dramatically suspicious. "Let me find a vase for those roses." She walks away from the counter and motions to Star that I am here before she walks to the back to find something.

I stare at my half eaten sandwich and coffee and sink to a feeling, one that feels as if I'm going to sleep on Christmas Eve to wake up to gifts galore. I pick up my flowers and smell them, getting lost in their floral scent. I couldn't help the flutter of my heart as the scent wafts through my body to jump start this feeling. Is this what I've actually been missing out on?

"I found this." Kassiah says, startling me out of my trance. She places an old vase in front of me that was probably in storage. "You can put your roses in there."

I nod as I try to get a piece of chicken out of my teeth. Anything to not make eye contact with Kassiah and the daggers she throws into my soul.

"I will after I eat." I pick up my sandwich and take another bite, still feeling the radiation of Kassiah's stare on me. Eventually, I can't take it anymore.

I cover my mouth and make eye contact with her expression, suspicious and confused. "Can I help you? Because I won't lie, the staring is pissing me off." I finish chewing and drop my hand from my mouth so she can see my frown.

"Rosen's showing up with flowers and gifts for you now?" Kassiah raises her eyebrow. "Is there something that you haven't told me about your last outing with Rosen?"

I haven't told Kassiah about the agreement we made because I couldn't tell her and hear about her giving me a lecture on how we should just be together. I can't imagine having my heart broken by my best friend. That would hurt more than anything. It's why I created the pact to be friends forever.

*My eyes widen when I slowly open them, realizing that the person behind the instant bliss was Rosen. His lips were soft against mine and tasted of the hot chocolate we drank at the winter dance just minutes ago. My heart beats in panic as I scan an undetectable look from Rosen's face.*

*"That was not supposed to happen." I stare down at the ground as if it can tell me how I went from telling my best friend good night to locking lips. I hope my mom and my sister are not looking at me through the window or something.*

*Rosen doesn't say anything to me, yet I can feel his eyes on me.*

*I look up at him, connecting our eyes. I put my pinky up to him, which causes a smile from his lips.*

*"What's that for?" He steps a little closer, looking at my lone finger.*

*"Promise me that we will always remain friends. I can't lose you."*

*Rosen sighs, "I didn't know I was such a bad kisser."*

*I push Rosen which causes him to laugh. "Please Rosen, I don't want us to make any mistakes like that again."*

*The smile has evaporated from his face. He stares at me, watching me intently before connecting pinkies with me. "I can't lose you, either."*

Rosen was not a bad kisser, he was my first, my best.

"Hello, earth to Kayani." Kassiah snaps as customers stand in front of me with books in their hands.

"I am so sorry." I say taking the books and ringing them up. I throw up free book marks before sending them out of the door. I wipe my hands on my apron as Kassiah scoffs at me.

"Something definitely happened, you better tell me right now." Kassiah walks over to the door and flips the on break sign, making sure no one comes in before I give her all the details.

"Nothing really happened. We just went to dinner."

"And somehow after dinner he ends up buying you dinner?"

I sigh, "So we went to dinner and the food was nasty, we went back to my place and had tacos."

"Please get to the good part." Kassiah motions for me to get on with the story.

I roll my eyes "So, one thing led to another and..."

"And y'all kissed again?" Kassiah asks, cutting me off, a small hint of a smirk forms on her lips.

"No. We didn't kiss." I regret telling Kassiah about that all those years ago. I had to beg her to stop asking me if we kissed or did anything of the sort whenever we hang out. It made me feel weird to even give Rosen a hug.

"So, what happened? Why is he bringing you flowers? Not that I am complaining or anything. You two definitely deserve each other."

I suddenly feel self-conscious. Do we really? Rosen has seen me cry after getting my heart broken and the things I told him men did to me. What if he is just buttering me up to make it worse. Grandma said to never tell a man about your past. Rosen has seen almost all of it with a front row seat.

I hug myself for comfort. "I told him about the horrible Valentine's Days and he said he wants to make me forget about it all."

Kassiah looks at me as if I was a new born baby, "Aww that is so sweet. There is a reason I always shipped you two together. He is the lover boy you need."

I shake my head, denying the comment which makes me feel wrong inside. "I think I'm okay."

Kassiah blows me off. "Girl please. The men you dated had you looking like an A1 dummy. Like, literally delusional."

"Delusional." I place my hand over my chest. Kassiah has always talked trash about the men I dated but not on me for dating them.

"Yes, delusional; you're over here convincing yourself that those men you dated were going to treat you like the ones in the books you read. You fell in love with those sweet meaningless words. The man they told you they were when you interrogate them through that 'getting to know you phase' and dream up the man he should be." She pauses, taking a sip of my coffee, which has probably turned cold by now. "When in reality, you have a man who is already willing to be that for you and more."

I shake my head "I can't."

"Ruin your friendship, I know, but how many times have you seen people have a happily ever after with their best friend?" Kassiah questions.

"Not enough to make me change my mind." I shrug.

"Come on, Kayani, are you really that blind? Rosen is crazy over you."

I laugh so hard my belly aches and a snort comes out of my nose. "What in the world makes you think that?"

"What dude schedules monthly dinners and doesn't let you pay? Fancy ones at that. And what man tells his best friend that he will give her a proper Valentine's Day?"

"Plenty of people have friends as Valentines," I wave her off. I've seen people in high school and college have one just so they won't feel left out. I always told Rosen not to get me anything, well I always had someone I thought would be a true Valentine for me at the time.

"And tell me, what best friend would go out of his way to plan dates, bring flowers and all, just to make your Valentine's pain go away?" Her eyebrows raise as she waits for my response.

"One that wants them to stop suffering."

Kassiah sighs, fed up with my denial, before turning over the sign on the door.

"Whatever, If you want to miss out on your prince charming, then be my guest"

# Chapter 5

I wait anxiously staring at the three little bubbles pop up on my screen. After my talk with Kassiah, Rosen has been at the front of my mind. I think back to that moment we agreed to this. The TV casted soft light against his face and a plethora of emotions on his face. I couldn't make out exactly what it was.

Best friends would do something like this right? I can't help but ask that question to myself the more I stare at the flowers on my table and think about the huge bear waiting for me upstairs. Rosen has won me bears before, has taken me to places multiple times, and has brought me food and snacks whenever I needed it. So what about this makes Kassiah think that this is romance other than it just being Valentine's season.

Delusional. That's all I can say about Kassiah's thoughts.

Rosen's message pops up on my screen, making my insides warm.

Okay

Sometimes I forget that Rosen has money and makes a lot of it. I only really remember when he takes me out to those fancy restaurants with the dress code or when Christmas rolls around and he gets me the most expensive gifts. The year I opened up my bookstore, he gave me an iPad when I was fine with a regular notebook from the store. The following year, I got him a game console after he told me how he had been stressed and could use an outlet. The last time Rosen played with a gaming system, his cousins broke it during a heated argument. I'll never forget that day.

Rosen and I also have access to each other's wishlists 24/7, so I always know what he wants, just in case.

I finish getting ready in something cute but cozy. Nothing says cute like a pair of warm leggings and a skirt with a cropped turtleneck. I put on my favorite vanilla perfume and complete my signature lip combo before picking out my ginger curls for a little more volume.

My phone lights up with a message from Kassiah.

Let me see the outfit (:

I pick up my phone and snap a picture, sending it to her. I told her about the plans today, even though It was against my better judgement; I couldn't let this outing go by without hearing my big sister's unsolicited advice.

I know that's right. Go get your man.

I roll my eyes at Kassiah's message as another one pops up from Rosen, letting me know the car is almost at my house. I grab the warmest coat I can find to wear before heading out.

He's not my man.

I send to Kassiah before I meet my ride outside of my house. A man dressed in a black tux smiles as I walk down the steps onto the pavement.

"Kayani?" The well groomed man asks as I approach. I nod, earning a bow from him as he opens the door.

"Your chariot awaits."

I enter the car and am enveloped in its warmth. Chocolates and champagne sit in the middle of the seating, waiting to be indulged. I fight the urge to kick my feet and scream like a schoolgirl. This is my best friend. I remind myself over and over but the wide grin that greets me as I stare into the rear view mirror would suggest otherwise.

***

As I make it to Rosen's apartment, I can smell the wax of a candle from outside the place. I knock on the door, shifting my weight between my legs as I wait for Rosen to appear behind the heavy gray door. A few moments later, he appears. His hair, as always, is looking freshly cut and his glasses are propped on his face. He leans against the threshold, a slight flex in his bicep with a slight smile as he runs his tongue against his bottom lip.

"Welcome." He says, before moving to the side to let me in.

My heart pounds, ignoring the look in his eyes that resembles hunger. I unzip my coat, feeling Rosen's gentle hands help ease me out of my coat. "Let me get that." His raspy voice rumbles through my body, making me regret the long sleeve shirt I put on. It's way too hot in here.

"It smells good in here." I cough a little, suddenly feeling a little dryness in my throat. "Are you burning candles?"

Rosen scratches the back of his neck. "Yeah, some type of cranberry cinnamon, I was going to get Lavender but the people at the store told me that makes people fall asleep."

I stare down at my feet so he can't see my smile. "My grandmother loved that scent."

He chuckles knowingly. I feel his presence closer and when I look up, he stands before me with a gentle gaze. "Follow me."

I let him lead me to the living room, where the culprit of the sweet smelling candles lie. They surround two easels with medium sized canvases. Behind them rest two fluffy pillows, and in the middle, a huge bottle of white wine (thank God it's not red) and a charcuterie board with cheese, grapes and pepperoni.

"I thought we could get started with a little painting and take a break when the food gets here." He pauses and looks down at my feet. "If that's cool."

He scratches behind his ear, donning a look of nervousness again; My smile spreads wider than it ever has before, and just from this moment alone, I know I'll need to invest in some facial cream to prevent smile lines.

"This is absolutely perfect. What kind of food did you order?"

"Chinese."

He chuckles when he sees my face light up from his response, "This is absolutely more than perfect."

We take our spots at the easels, the paints lay before each of our stations, along with paint brushes and little cups of water. My smile still has not erased and I don't think it has since I stepped into that cab.

"How was the ride over?" Rosen asks as he opens up his paints.

"It was very warm." I roll up my sleeves as I open my paint. Focusing on only coloring number one.

"Good. I told Kenny to make sure it was extra warm for you."

If I could smile more I could. "You are so sweet, you know that?" Rosen shrugs as he paints, his arm flexing a little as he strokes his brush against the canvas.

"It's all part of what I'm trying to show you this week." He pauses before clapping his hands. Instantly, the fireplace sparks and slow jazz music starts to play in the background. "Took me all morning to figure out that command." He chuckles.

"What exactly are you trying to show me?" I turn my attention back to my canvas, focusing on the stroke of my brush.

"Anyone can wine and dine you and give you flowers, Kayani. It's the little things that make a difference in showing you love someone."

I stop mid stroke as I work blue paint onto my canvas. "Explain."

He lets out a sigh of longing as he continues to paint. "It's knowing what they need just by their body language. Knowing just the right amount of pressure to give them in a hug to make them feel safe. Knowing that tulips on the table in the morning will remind her of sweet things from her past. Exactly where to kiss her to make her feel like she's always been this loved."

Rosen and I connect eyes, paint dripping on the wood of his easel. My breath slows rapidly as we stare into each other's eyes.

"And how would a person know that this is love?" I ask slowly.

"You just know." He chuckles lowly, turning his attention back to the painting, dipping his paint brush back into the red paint.

I turn back to the mostly white picture in front of me, processing the words Rosen has shared with me. It tugged at my heart strings more than anything he has told me before. I stare in shock, figuring out this feeling that envelops me as I sit here next to him.

"You okay?" Rosen questions, snapping me out of my trance.

"Yes." I say, putting my paint brush down and getting up suddenly. "Just need to use the bathroom."

I walk down Rosen's narrow hallway until I find the bathroom. I close the door and lean my body against it, putting my hands over my pounding heart as a joyous smile overcomes my lips. I walk to the sink and stare at myself in the mirror. I'd be lying if I didn't see the glow within me. Does love also cause this? I splash water on my face before staring at myself. I squeal silently preparing myself to exit and face this man.

***

### *Rosen*

The chinese comes while Kayani is in the bathroom. I set up the food in takeout bowls that I picked up at the store the other day. I set up her food and sauces by her canvas and change the station on the radio to something with more substance. Jazz makes me want to fall asleep sometimes. I sit on my pillow just as Kayani comes back. That smile of hers has barely left her face since she got here and that just proves I'm doing a better job at this than I thought. With everything on the list, I know she's going to love each coming day better than this one. "You okay?" I ask as she sits down next to me. Her smile widens again when she sees the ceramic chinese take out shaped bowls. "You're going to have my face wrinkly being with you." She says as she picks up the bowl, pouring duck sauce over her rice and chicken. With you. Her words make my heart jump, knowing that she probably just means being around me but it still gives me hope. Maybe she can finally see what I've been trying to subtly tell her all these years. "I just remember when you always admired how people on TV could always eat out of the containers and you couldn't." I chuckle. "Yeah, I always have to share with others." She shoots me a dirty look before taking a bite of her food. "I think that look was meant for your mom and sister." I laugh. "You're the one who likes the same chinese order as me." Her voice gets a little loud as she defends herself. "It's not my fault you changed me. General tso's chicken and shrimp fried rice is an elite combo." She squints her eyes at me before shrugging. "What can I say, I guess I'm an influencer." We laugh before sharing comfortable silence as we eat, painting here and there as R&B plays in the background. Our song starts to play on the radio, making Kayani start to dance as she chews her food.I place my bowl down and begin to paint, watching Kayani wind her hips from my peripheral vision. She hums sweetly to the song as the chorus starts to play. I reach over and grab the wine bottle, pouring the white wine in our glasses. I start to smile when she starts to sing audibly, letting the melody of her voice serenade me. My favorite part comes on, making me and Kayani sing in Harmony. We stare into each other's eyes as we sing the lines. "You don't know I can't live without you, baby." We harmonize together. We share laughter as we take a sip of wine from the glass. "You still think you can sing, huh?" Kayani jokes, peeking at me over the top of her wine glass."I think I got better. I may not sing as sweetly as you, but I got vocals." I puff my chest proudly and put the glass down."How was work today?" Kayani asks, changing the subject."It was fine. I have a meeting with the boss. New restaurant to try in a few days.""Wow, two restaurants in one month?" She teases. "Think of this as a part of your week." I shrug and continue to paint."You know I don't have a dress to wear." Kayani laughs. "I think you look beautiful in anything." She glows against the fireplace, the cranberry mixed with her signature vanilla scent smells heavenly right now. "Anything?" She questions as if she doesn't believe me. Like I haven't seen her on her worst days. In her sweatpants and messy bun. When she throws on mix match socks and crazy clothing combos to walk to the corner store. I've seen when she practiced doing her own makeup, using the wrong foundation. I turn my body toward her, giving her my attention. "Yes, beauty is in the eye of the beholder."She smiles at those words, proving my point further "I love when you wear green. Sage green, particularly. Or purple." Though she hates wearing purple, because the ginger of her natural hair makes her feel like a PB&J, just like wearing black makes her think of halloween. But all I see is beauty.Her eyes twinkle a little as she stares at me. "I have one green dress."I open my mouth to tell her it's my favorite, but advise against it. This should be friendly, instead I'm telling her about how beautiful she is in certain colors. "I'll get you a dress for the occasion." "You don't have to spoil me with the material things." Her whole presence seems ethereal, "This is enough." I nod, "I know you will look beautiful in anything you wear. Rewear a dress, this is a new restaurant.""But the people are bougie." She pouts. I chuckle. "And we aren't?"She faces her body toward me, "I'm just waiting for you to show me what you are going to do on the actual day." She giggles.My heart leaps hearing those words. "Are you looking forward to Valentine's Day?" I smirk.She freezes before a small smirk appears on her face. "I wouldn't say looking forward, just curious." "You can be excited for something, it's okay." I reach over and grab her hand, "Your heart is safe with me." She nods "Yes, and that's what's scary.""How so?" I wouldn't lie and say I'm not scared, too. Doing all this for a woman, who after the 14th, will place me right back to what we previously were - friends. And that's scary to me. Showing her she's worth more and not being good enough myself. "Your heart could be in the most gentle hands and still break." She pauses, "People are only gentle for so long."I tilt my head. "Do you think you can break If you were in my hands?" Her eyes slowly reach mine. "No, but."I shake my head, cutting her off. "You fill your head with so much. Go in trusting me blindly. I know it's hard, but I'll guide you.""Trust you for how long?" She questions."That's up to you."We sit in silence, not taking our eyes off of each other as Musiq Soulchild plays softly in the background. "You know." She says, breaking the silence. "I don't think I'll be finishing my painting tonight." I run my tongue across my bottom lips "Me, too." She rolls her eyes, which makes me laugh. "Did I do something wrong?""You keep licking your lips." "I did it once." I laugh."Twice." She plays with one of her curls as she rolls her eyes again."And you're keeping track? Do you find that attractive?" She makes eye contact with me again, I purposely lick my lip again. "Boy, you wish.""Don't tell me you still think about these lips after all these years." I say.If Kayani could turn red, she'd be a fireball right now. She grabs her paintbrush and lunges at me, threatening to paint my face a shade of blue"Did I embarrass you?" I ask as she holds the brush close to my face."Rosen, I'm not playing with you." She unsuccessfully tries to force the brush closer to my face. My gaze goes from the paint covered brush to her beautiful face. Her curls surround her face beautifully, making her impossible not to look at. I smirk and place one of my hands on her hip, my thumb grazing the soft skin of her waist line. She jumps back, a loud thud sounding as she lands on her butt."My hands cold?" I sit up and watch her face, and she grabs the huge wine glass, drinking the last of her white wine. "You are too much." She says quietly. She grabs the bottle and pours a lot more wine in her glass. As I move, she flinches and sits on her pillow, her face flushed from my touch."What are you thinking?" I ask as she picks up her paintbrush and drinks her wine while she paints. Something tells me she is painting the wrong spots."Do you have to remind yourself that we're only friends?" My eyes widen at her statement. A new hunger fills her eyes as she looks at me. I nod slowly and pick up my wine glass, taking a sip. "All the time." She gives me a look I can't quite pinpoint as The Isley Brothers play in the background. The glow from the fireplace and candles is the only light filling the space around us. I hold up my wine glass, "Cheers to being the best of friends." Kayani opens her mouth to speak but decides against it. "Cheers." She says, clinking her glass with mine.We slowly retract our glasses and sip to our friendship, staring at each other much differently over the top of our drinks.

# Chapter 6



"If we can get Mr. Harbough to invest in..." My thoughts daze as I sit in this board meeting, uninterested in the words that spill out of Mr. Brown's mouth. I usually am always attentive, jotting down notes and ready to be the first one to reach out to clients for a meeting. But I've done that already, and this client won't invest in anything but his future, which is respectable. I help people manage their money, but my boss is always looking for ways to expand their money because it'll be more for us in the long run. I'm not interested in that, however, I just do what's in my job description and I do one heck of a job at it.

I stare down at the blank white notepad that I brought with me, feeling as if I should doodle Kayani's name on it with hearts, since she's what I'm thinking about. But, she always is. I stare down at my hand tattoo. The one that I got when I was 18 and regretted it afterwards because it was a rose. At first, when I got the tattoo, it was for my mom, who would call me her rose sometimes. But that meaning has changed over time, or at least I tried to change it into something with meaning. My mom's name is already etched into my collarbone. She's the first woman close to my heart. You think Kayani would be creeped out or gross if I put her name on the other side?

"Alright guys, so do we have a deal? The plan is simple." Mr. Brown asks, standing with his back straight, making his protruding belly stick out.

I look around confused as everyone nods their head in agreement. I flick my hand into the air, trying to sound confident about my lack of knowing what's going on.

"Sorry sir, What is the plan? I was just thinking about how we could get Mr. Harbough on board. I do meet with him for lunch this week."

Mr. Brown nods his head. "Ah yes, the lunch, about that." He begins before turning around to the rest of the team at the table.

"You guys can go, I want to have a quick chat with one of our star accountants." With a wave of his hand, he dismisses everyone. Mr. Brown has no problem praising people for doing a good job. It's one of the reasons we are top of the list, everyone wants to earn Mr. Brown's approval.

"So, what's going on today, Mr. Brown?" I say, closing my laptop that has the shared presentation loaded up. "I wanted to ask if you could do something bigger than lunch with this particular client." He asks as he takes out the chair next to me to have a seat. "Bigger than lunch?" The first thing that comes to mind is sending this guy a gift basket. Who doesn't love baked goods?

"A lot of clients rave about your charm and your lunch appointments, but I want to take things a step further."

I lean forward, intrigued. "I'm listening.

"Mr. Harbough has a nonprofit organization and there is an event this week, I think the 14th."

My heart drops at the statement. A work trip for Valentine's day?

"Valentine's Day?" I ask, my throat a little dry. I left my water back on my desk.

"Yes, Valentine's day. A spread the love event, he's partnering with a charity. Anyway I put your name on the list."

Great, so even If I wanted to back out, I can't.

"You're single, right? No plans." He points to my empty finger, seeing no wedding band. Before I can answer and tell him I did have plans for that whole day, he stands up abruptly. "Great, I'll send over the flight and hotel Information."

"It's already paid for?" I ask, confused. I think of the people in this room who were supposed to go to this event. I know traveling is a part of the job, but this is one commitment I don't think I can do, unless there is another way.

"Yes, I was going to go but that's Valentine's Day, the misses wouldn't like that." He chuckles before he pats my back and leaves the room.

My phone dings, singaling my flowers have arrived to Kayani at work today. I grab my items and think overtime of how I can make this Valentine's Day special for her if work is in the way.

After my last meeting of the day, I decided to go home and start setting up my date with Kayani. I sent her a bouquet of flowers, Tulips this time, to ease off the romance of roses for a little bit, and attached a note to be at my place as soon as she gets off, which should be in a couple hours.

I got groceries to be delivered to my house in about two hours time; I planned on cooking her dinner tonight, something different but equally as intimate. As I take the elevator up to my apartment, my mind can't stop trying to figure out what to do for Valentine's day, now that it won't be spent in our home town. Once I got into my apartment, I threw my items on the couch, loosened my tie, and opened up my personal laptop to see the information my boss had about the hotels. \

It's a nice hotel, considering my boss paid for it. I would've gone the cheaper route, just because I like to spend my money on city luxuries, and hotels don't really scream luxury to me. Whenever I'm working my butt off for the boss man, I could sleep on concrete and it would feel like a cloud after the various meetings and events I attend on these trips. I stare at the details and type in the hotel names to look at pictures of the rooms. Some of them are nice with city views and perfect scenery from the balconies.

As I stare at the city view in the picture, an idea pops into my head. One far more luxurious than the hotel in front of me. I open up a blank document and write down all the things I need to make this idea of mine a reality.

My phone pings, signaling my groceries are going to be delivered shortly, which reminds me to set reservations for dinner tomorrow. I smile, seeing my plan come to fruition.

***

### Kayani

"So, how are things with Rosen, he confess his love yet?" Kassiah asks behind the counter as she watches me stock books onto my shelves.

"Rosen and I are just friends." I've been telling myself that for the past 24 hours, especially when I reminisce on the things Rosen said to me. The way he looked at me as we sipped wine and painted pictures, which we spent all night trying to finish. His gentle touch on my skin when I threatened to paint his face. It all felt so different... Seeing him with the glow of the fireplace and candle light. It makes me feel warm, warmer than a friend should feel.

"You say that, yet he sends another bouquet of flowers." Kassiah says, looking at the rose and white tulip combination next to her.

Kassiah's eyes lit when she saw the huge smile on my face when I got them. The bouquet was huge and shaped in a large circle.

"What girl doesn't like getting flowers." I shrug. "It's a part of the thing he's trying to show me."

"And what is he trying to show you?" Kassiah asks, sending me into a spiral.

*"Anyone can wine and dine you and give you flowers, Kayani. It's the little things that make a difference in showing you love someone..."*

*I stop mid stroke as I work blue paint onto my canvas. "Explain."*

*He lets out a sigh of longing as he continues to paint. "It's knowing what they need just by their body language. Knowing just the right amount of pressure to give them in a hug to make them feel safe. Knowing that tulips on the table in the morning will remind her of sweet things from her past. Exactly where to kiss her to make her feel like she's always been this loved."*

*Rosen and I connect eyes, Paint drips on the wood of his easel. My breath slows rapidly as we stare into each other's eyes.*

*"And how would a person know that this is love?" I ask slowly.*

*"You just know." He chuckles lowly, turning his attention back to the painting, dipping his paint brush back into the red paint.*

I fight the urge to squeal again at the memory, instead, I turn away from Kassiah so that my back faces her completely and smile to myself.

"He just wants to make up for all the bad Valentine's Days I've had." I continue to slowly stock the books on the shelf.

"And you still think he's not in love." Kassiah laughs, "Yeah right."

I shrug again, not paying Kassiah any mind. One big difference about Kassiah and I is that she likes to express herself and let it be known. I think, because she's my older sister, it's natural for her, but with me, I'm used to hiding my feelings. Not that there is anything to hide, it's just with Rosen, it already feels natural to be his friend, I don't want to ruin what we have spent so long creating.

"So, what does lover boy have planned today?" she asks as she flips her braids over her shoulder and scrolls through her phone. Kassiah works from home, which also keeps me from hiring someone else at the shop; she does both jobs at the same time. It's one hell of a realistic greenscreen for the video calls.

"I don't know, he texted me to come by today." I wipe my hands on my apron and look at the bouquet of flowers in front of me. It feels as if I'm walking through a rose garden these days, with the amount of flowers I have between my house and the bookstore. This is definitely one thing I can get used to.

"Mhm. Well don't forget the plans that we also have with Star. She is really excited about her gift for you this year." Her pearly whites shine against the harsh lighting.

"I know it's good then, if you're smiling like this." Knowing my sister, she probably had a whole say in my gift. Can everyone tell how miserable I am around this holiday?

"Whatever, at least you're not moping around anymore. But I will be moping if you don't go home and change into something more perfect for your man."

I look down at my jeans and fluffy boots, not to mention my caramel colored sweater that I raved to Kassiah about how soft it was when I bought it.

"I look fine." I did my curls in a big voluminous way, just how I like it.

"Not fine enough." Kassiah comes out from behind the counter and grabs my apron. "You do yourself a favor and go get cute. I will man down the fort."

I roll my eyes and give up my apron before grabbing my keys. "Can you finish my to-do list?"

She nods before practically shoving me out of the door. I look up at the cloudy sky, the air smells of rain, and I sigh as I walk the few blocks to my house.


I opted out of my jeans for a long sleeve red dress and some sheer leggings. The dress stops at mid thigh and to dress it down, I put my fuzzy black boots on from earlier and a cute headband. Kassiah closed up for me, which I need to thank her for holding it down for me this week with a sister dinner or something. I know she loves when I cook Baked Ziti.

Around 6 is when I arrive at Rosen's apartment, I can't help but fight a pile of butterflies when I get to his place. I haven't been at his place that much, but twice in the last few days feels a bit overwhelming. Like I'm the girlfriend who is always around. It feels that way as I walk down this hallway and wave to the lingering strangers making their way to their apartments with their fake smiles, it's almost like they're mocking me. That they know the real reason why I'm here.

I arrive at Rosen's door and knock swiftly. My knuckles tap the hard wood as I wait outside, paranoid. I feel like an imposter. I caught myself earlier, not defending myself against Kassiah's description of Rosen as *my man,* which, let's face it, If he was, I'd throw on something better than this. But a slither of me is thinking that I can't be showing up here as his friend.

Rosen opens the door and the smell of candles and aromatic cooking leaves my nerves at a blissful peace. He stands in front of me in gray jeans and a button down black shirt. He's wearing those glasses again, which makes my heart knock waves of speckled excitement through my body.

"You look good in red." He smiles as he moves to the side, letting me in.

"Thank you." It's all I manage to speak, I can't seem to get my usual banter going with Rosen. Not after his model appearance at the front door. Not with the laser focused gaze I feel of his on my back side. I take in a deep breath as I continue to walk through the apartment. The smell of yesterday's candle lingers, but something else catches my attention.

Piles of ingredients cover the island in Rosen's kitchen. The oven is slowly preheating to the perfect temperature and the smell of sauteed vegetables is barely noticeable under the smell of the candles. I stare in awe as Rosen appears before me again, tying an apron around his waist.

"Are you cooking for me?" I ask, walking over to the kitchen to survey the ingredients. I spot chocolate cheesecake on the counter, one of my favorite desserts.

A hearty chuckle comes from Rosen, making my insides melt. "Yes, I felt bad for our crab cake fiasco and thought I would make you some."

I stand taken aback. Rosen. Is. Making. Me. Crab Cakes.

My head shakes profusely as Rosen turns to put the already made crab balls in the oven. "Is that all you had planned?"

This question makes me feel stupid. It's Rosen, of course this isn't what he had planned.

"No, but come closer, I don't want you to get a glimpse of the living room yet." He says. I walk closer, seeing one of the pots on the stove belong to a big heap of mashed potatoes, my favorite. And a pan of vegetables.

I move closer to Rosen, feeling compelled to him. Feeling the urge to, to...

"Are you okay?" Rosen asks as he stands tall again. His hands on my waist to stop me from walking any closer to him. His hands feel like they were made for my body. His touch is delicate, yet lights a fire inside of me. I look up into Rosen's dreamy expression, looking into the chocolate orbs of his eyes before I nod.

He chuckles and grabs my hand. "Those will take a little while to bake, so let me show you my next surprise."

In the living room before me is a makeshift fort from pillows and blankets. I didn't know Rosen had this many, because you know...Men. We used to make forts all the time at his mom's house because we knew better at my house.

"You made us a fort." The laughter eases my one sided tension as I sink to my knees to look at the details.

I look up to see Rosen's eyes on me, his gaze is heavy. From this angle, I can see the slow rise and fall of his chest.

"Look inside." His smile rises to one side of his face. I pull back the flaps to see fuzzy blankets and two romance novels, not just any, but one that I had on my list. They sit in front of my makeshift seat with bows on top. Across is the book Rosen bought the other day, and a bowl of chips sit in between the space. Little tea lights fill the ambiance of fake candles, and rose petals cover the ground.

I take my head out of the space and look up at Rosen. "Are we?"

"Buddy reading? Or read-a-thoning? I thought it would be good after dinner to just read together."

I ball my fist to keep my hands from shaking. "Why?"

"Why what?" He gets down on the ground next to me. When I don't look at him, he places a hand on my thigh, earning the attention he deserves.

"What made you want to read with me?" I laugh to keep the tears from falling.

He turns my face toward him, I instantly get lost in those dark eyes. Feeling as if I'm floating in an infinite sea. "I want to get lost in your world for a change."

"My world?" I push a loose curl behind my ear.

"The love life you swear exists in those pages. I want to see if maybe." He shrugs. "I can help you live in one." He stands, leaving me there stunned at his words. The words that basically started it all, the words that had me agreeing to a love I didn't know existed.

After dinner, Rosen and I turned off his apartment lights and let the only light shine from the makeshift fort he made for us. The crab cakes were so good, I can tell he got the recipe from his mom, and I am 100% not complaining. I love her food. I snuggle under my blanket he left for me and pick up one of the books that he got for me to read.

I peek over at Rosen who is already reading. He wears his glasses again, which is my favorite side of Rosen. It makes him look smarter. He wets his bottom lip with his tongue and turns his head to look at the next page, "I can feel you staring." He looks up at me, the tealight by his eyes gives a warm glow to them as they scan every inch of my face and body.

"I'm sorry. I just have a lot on my mind." Which isn't a lie but he looks better than the words in this book right now.

"Can't read in front of me?" He smirks

I laugh. "I did already."

He shrugs and puts the book down. "What's on your mind?"

"What do you have planned for tomorrow.?" I ask.

"Dinner, but at a restaurant. I have a busy day tomorrow but I want to end it with you."

I smile "You've been ending it with me a lot these past few days."

"Just like the old days." He winks.

When Rosen and I were younger, we used to talk on the phone until we both fell asleep or sneak out to meet at the park when we both couldn't sleep. This reminds me of that and it's probably why I have been having the best sleep of my life while dreaming of him.

"Rosen, you ever think about our friendship?" I blurt out.

"All the time, but what specifically about it?" He asks.

"How it changed over the years."

"Good or bad?"

A silence lingers between us as he waits for my response. "Good." I squeak out. My eyes dart to the fuzzy tan blankets before me, the chips in the center of us. Anything but his face.

"I think about the good, too, but what makes you say that?"

I can hear the fear in his voice, as if he thinks I'm going to stop being friends with him because of this. But being friends somehow doesn't feel enough. "Do you feel it changing now?"

I force myself to meet his eyes and this sends a small smile to his face. "Yes, but it's your choice."

He looks back down at his book. I let out a shaky breath and open the first page of my book. I sneak one last look at him before reading the first words on the page

*He is everything I could ever want and more.*

# Chapter 7

*Rosen*

Before dinner, we walk, working up an appetite. Also trying to erase my mind of Kayani in this beautiful green dress. The color on her just does something to me. It compliments her perfect brown skin so elegantly. She shows me up with that color every time she wears it. Our reservation isn't for another thirty minutes or so, but I couldn't help but see Kayani a little earlier.

My Valentine's plan goes into effect today and I'm just hoping she says yes to it after all. I spent the last few days trying to plan everything I need for Valentine's Day. It almost feels like I'm proposing, I know I'll have to top this when I finally get Kayani to be mine.

"It's a good thing you had slides in your car." Kayani says, the rubber soles slapping the pavement as we walk slowly. The slides are way too big for her feet.

"My gym bag is always in my car." I chuckle, clenching and unclenching my hand into a fist to stop myself from touching her.

"Well, I thank you, I can only walk for so long in heels." She gives me a smile before looking around the downtown area to see the new stores and the old ones we like so much.

I stare at her ginger hair, smelling the fruity products she puts in her curls when a gentle breeze passes. I smile when she looks in awe at some of the new shops. This area is the best when it comes to Christmas, they make it almost like Santa's village.

"So, can I ask you something?" I ask Kayani as we continue to walk down the street.

"Yes?" She says, stopping in front of a light pole, allowing honey rays to fall into her pupils.

"Am I doing a good job at, you know." I pause shifting my stance. "Making you forget about your past ills about Valentine's day."

Her smile grows slowly, and she nods matter of factly "I think you're doing an amazing job. I think everything you did feels good."

"Feels good?" My heart leaps hearing the words. It's what I want her to feel all the time. Good, But I want to make her feel even better than good. I want her to feel amazing.

We continue to walk slowly, making our way to a sort of busy intersection. The street lights begin to shine as hues of pink and red lights begin to stretch out across the sky. The setting sun making the night come alive.

"It feels good to be loved, to be shown properly. This feels like every other day I have with you just, it feels more."

I smile, although this feels like another friend zone stint, which I am trying to get out of. Part of the reason Kayani and I haven't been able to hang out as we do is because of our schedules. Me with work and her with work and throwing events with her store and traveling. I honestly think we could've been an item, if we both weren't so busy.

"Do you get it, though? The type of things you deserve?"

She smiles "I think I do. Definitely raised my standards. I don't think anyone can top that."

I smile triumphantly.

"What?" She smacks my arm playfully. "What's so funny?"

"Nothing, this is just what real lover boys do." I shrug. "Maybe I don't want anyone to top what I can do for you."

Those words make her eyes soften. It's almost like she's open to the idea of us every time we're together. Something I've been dreaming about since high school.

"Of course nobody can top you. You know me like the back of your hand." I grab Kayanis hand and carefully walk her across the street when the traffic is on our side and continue to walk the path illuminated by the stores.

"As a lover should. I should know what triggers you, what makes you laugh and smile. I should be open to trying new things that I don't really enjoy because it makes you happy. I think you deserve a lover like that."

"So, you think I deserve you?" Kayani asks, a look or longing on her face. I open my mouth to say yes but I'm too scared of what that answer would yield me.

"I think you deserve the love your heart desires."

Kayani opens her mouth to speak but gets side tracked to a small boutique across the street. I can see by the glass in the store behind her, a beautiful purple dress has caught her attention.

I look down at her, relieved and sad by our shift in conversation. "You want to go to the seamstress?" I ask.

Before I even have a chance to say anything else, she grabs my hand to drag me across the street, straight to the dress that is displayed in the showcase.

"Rosen," She gasps as she reaches the glass case. "This is so beautiful."

I chuckle "Do you want to go in?"

Just as Kayani opens her mouth, the woman in the shop comes out to greet us. "Hi, I couldn't help but see you guys from the window." She says, smiling. Her dark brown hair is styled in a pixie cut, she glows from the joy of seeing us admire her work.

"I think she would like to come in, if that's cool with you." I chuckle.

She nods vigorously, ushering us in. I grab Kayani's hand and lead her inside the small boutique, where so many dresses fill the space.

"Please, don't be shy." She says, making Kayani let go of my hand and explore the space. She looks like she's in a trance. A wonderland of thoughts as she surveys the array of dresses. I just stand and watch in awe. Like when she's in a bookstore or at a bakery we frequent sometimes. Seeing her in new elements, in new spaces, makes it hard not to fall for her.

When Kayani stands on the other side of the shop, I sneak my way over to the women who greeted us.

"Hi, How much is that dress outside in the case." I look back to make sure Kayani does not see me.

The woman smiles ear to ear. She totals up the dress and I slip her my card. "Can I pick it up tomorrow?"

She nods enthusiastically as she hands me my card back. This dress would go perfect for her Valentine's Day surprise.

Kayani comes back to me, a small smile spreading across her face. "Everything in here is beautiful, but my wallet is screaming at me." She giggles a little.

"Did you see anything you like?"

I wish I could follow her around the store. And buy every dress she touches. She would look beautiful in that baby yellow satin dress in the corner or the baby blue gown with the thigh slit displayed front and center in the store. She is the princess made for all of these. The woman made for a soft life.

She grabs my face, looking up at me, locking me in with her eyes and glossy lips. "There's a lot of dresses I love but we're going to miss our dinner reservation."

It's almost like she can tell when I want to spoil her. As if I don't do it a lot already. I scan her eyes, realizing the seriousness to it before putting my forehead against hers.

'Fine, but don't hold back next time."

She laughs and pushes me away. The woman behind the counter comes out to wish us a good night.

"You guys are such a beautiful couple. I hope you enjoy your dinner."

Kayani's face flushes as she opens her mouth for words but nothing comes to her. I laugh and wave a good night before leading Kayani back out into the cool air.

"Let's get to dinner." Kayani halts.

I turn to her confused. "That woman called us a couple, you weren't going to say anything?"

I can see the confusion across her own face. Her gaze at me looks as if she's in a past memory. One that I hope I can eliminate tonight.

"I'd be honored if someone calls you my girl. It's a compliment."

She looks even more confused but I don't stop to hear her new thoughts. I take her hand gently and walk her back to the car so she can grab her heels and we can go to the restaurant. I wipe my free hand along my suit jacket, hoping tonight goes as planned.

***

*Kayani*

As Rosen walks with me side by side to the restaurant, I can't help but recall his words.

*"I'd be honored if someone calls you my girl. It's a compliment."*

Those words have me quiet, still quiet, as Rosen speaks to the host before they lead us to our table. The area is softly lit, candles mostly fill in the light around us. Soft chatter and the clinks of utensils against porcelain fill the space.

At the front, a small stage appears, lit by soft stage lighting, a single piano standing in the middle of the stage.

"Taking me to places with live music now, huh?" I ask in an attempt to make a joke. Rosen looks at me halfway over his shoulder. I can only see a hint of a smile.

"I try to take you to places you've never been." He chuckles as we reach our table. He pulls the chair out for me and pushes me in before sitting across.

The low lighting does nothing but justice for him as he stares at me, a huge smile on his face as he looks at me with love in his eyes. Well, what I believe to be love.

"Are you getting crab cakes?" Rosen asks as he looks at the menu.

"I think I will go for the lobster dinner."

Rosen's head shoots up as he looks at me with a intrigued expression.

"Really?" He leans forward, calling my bluff.

"Yes, actually. I think it's good to go for a change." I say, putting the menu to the side with my mind made up.

He smirks and closes his menu. "I like that. I think I will, too, then."

We both smile as the waiter comes up to us to take our orders. "What can I get you guys today?"

"Two lobster dinners." Rosen says, catching my eye to make sure it's what I want. I give him a small nod as he turns back to the waiter.

"And to drink?"

"White."

"Red." I say cutting Rosen off, earning another look from him.

"Red wine. Your best." he says. The waiter grabs our menus before walking away.

"Who is this new Kayani?" Rosen leans forward, his eyebrows wiggling.

I try not to laugh too loudly before grabbing my napkin and placing it on my lap. "I just think it's time to try new things. I technically have been all week."

Rosen's posture relaxes as the waiter comes out and pours red wine in our glasses. "To new things." He lifts his glass and we lightly tap rims before taking a sip.

The waiter smiles, waiting for compliments of his wine choice. The red wine is sweet, just how I like mine.

"This is really good." I say, looking inside the glass, seeing what kind of magic they put in this. "When is the music playing, so I can sip my wine to the symphony?" I joke

"Sorry, but there is no live music tonight." The waiter frowns, "Our pianist is sick."

"Aww." I poke my bottom lip in a pout, looking at Rosen.

He smirks and gets up from his chair. "May I?" He asks the waiter, waving his hands in the direction of the stage.

With a swift nod, I watch Rosen get up on stage in front of the piano. I want to cover my face in embarrassment, not knowing when the last time Rosen played the piano, or if he knows more than just the one he played for his parents' anniversary.

People start to stare as Rosen sits on the bench and moves the microphone in front of his lips. God I hope he doesn't sing. We both know he can't.

"Good Evening, ladies and gentlemen. I'm sorry there is no live music tonight. I know my date and I were both looking forward to it."

A murmur of whispers flows through the crowd, all agreeing with the disappointment.

"With Valentine's Day quickly approaching, I wanted to play a love song for all the couples in the room. And to the future ones." Rosen looks at me and winks, sending butterflies through my chest.

It's quiet, not a whisper or fork hits the plate as Rosen cracks his knuckles. He closes his eyes as he begins to hit the keys, playing John Legend's "All of me".

People smile as the keys serenade the place. I watch as Rosen meticulously places his fingers over each key, hitting each one with the amount of force to give us this beautiful memory. This song he played for everyone. For the couples, the singles, for me.

There's no denying what I feel now, as the melody pulls out the words my heart wants to sing. I want to tell Rosen that I know what it's like to be loved, that I know now what it should feel like because it's like that every second with him. It's been that way since we were kids, playing tag and making up adventures in our yards, since the late nights we would stay up and sneak out to see each other. Since that kiss on the porch in high school. When I was too afraid to tell him how I felt after all this time.

When the melody stops, my heart is full. Our food has been placed in front of us. A standing ovation roars from the crowd as Rosen bows. I wave my eyes dry, trying not to cry in front of strangers.

Rosen shakes hands with people as he gets off stage and makes his way over to me. God, this feels like a moment where he should propose to me. He sits down in front of me with a nervous smile on his face.

"I see the food has come." He wipes his hands on the napkin before placing it on his lap.

I nod, unable to speak. A fear I might cry.

"I have something I want to talk to you about, Kayani." Rosen lets out a shaky sigh.

My heart beats in my chest as I wait for him to respond. He takes a sip of the wine before him.

"My boss asked me to go on a business trip for a client." He pauses another sigh leaving his body. "On Valentine's Day."

My shoulders slump at the news. "Oh."

He nods. "But I can't do that. I can't live up to making promises to you and then dropping the ball."

My heart thuds in my chest "I understand, work is work."

I stare down at my perfectly cooked lobster and vegetables.

"I want you to come with me, Kayani. Spend Valentine's with me in New York."

I look up at Rosen, that smile still there. Confidence breeding from his shoulders.

"Really?" I ask.

"I already bought the plane tickets. We leave tomorrow. I know it's last minute, but I wanted to tell you over dinner and hopefully..."

"Yes." I say, not letting him finish, no other thought is needed.

"You serious?"

"Kassiah can hold down the bookstore for me. Plus, you said you'd show me this week, right? Let's just call this a part of your plans that you have for me." I smile and take a sip of my wine.

"I was hoping you'd see it that way." He lets out a long sigh of relief.

"I'm your best friend, of course I would see it that way." Those words tasted bitter in my mouth. Best friends – I don't think that fits us anymore. I think something more needs to be established.

He laughs, a little dry. "Yeah, of course."

I pick at my food and eat a few pieces of veggie. "I'm going to have to pack my gift for you." I say, thinking of the gifts that I wanted to get Rosen but have definitely not picked out yet.

He chuckles. "You don't have to. I can wait til we get back. The day is about you."

I shake my head. "I want for things to be reciprocated."

Our eyes connect, his lips tug before he stares at his plate with a shadow of a smile.

"Unless you want to get your gift during side chick day. I mean, I had something like that happen, too."

He laughs. "You always get the short end of the stick, huh. I think maybe this needs to continue after Valentine's Day. You don't have good luck with men."

I giggle. "I think I do now, though." Not too many girls can find someone who will serenade them in front of a restaurant. Change the plans so that it doesn't end in disappointment but something better. At least, that's what I hope Valentine's day with him will feel like.

Every girl doesn't need to settle for Mr. Bare minimum or below basic. But someone who will make every heartache feel as if it was only a scratch. That the right love from the right person heals all wounds.

He winks at me and nods toward my Lobster. "Found someone that will take you to get Lobster and red wine? You know I knew a girl who used to hate red wine."

"Oh really, why is that?" I ask, already knowing the answer.

"She hated it around the 14th of February. Too romantic. I wonder what she thinks of it now."

I take a sip of the red wine. "I think she can get used to this."

"I can drink to that." Rosen says, taking a sip. We both give each other a knowing look over the rim of our glasses.

# Chapter 8



"But Auntie, Valentine's Day is tomorrow." Star says to me as she looks at the gift bags that I hand over to her.

Her eyes droop as her lip pouts, staring at the bags.

"I know, but Auntie is going away for Valentine's Day this year." I drop down to her height and fluff out one of the two huge puffs in her hair.

"Okay." She looks at the bags one more time. "I won't open them until tomorrow." She sticks out her small pinky as a promise, which I accept wrapping my pinky around hers.

"I think I did my big one this year." I smile before standing up straight. "Put those bags down and help me pack." I say.

She smiles at this, placing the bags on my couch before running upstairs to my bedroom. Kassiah smiles at me, a look I can't pinpoint showing on her face.

"I want to hear all about the trip. When you get back."

I rock on the heels of my feet, feeling like a bomb waiting to tick. I let out a deep breath. "Kassiah, you were right. Well, are right."

Her eyebrow raises as she slowly takes a seat on the arm of my couch. "Right about what? That you should be packing since your flight leaves later tonight?"

I shake my head "No, you are right about Rosen. I really really like him."

Kassiah's smile stretches ear to ear, she stands up and claps her hands excitedly. "I told you! And this isn't a 'like like' situation. I'm your older sister, I know you love him."

I hide my face, wishing the sun was back in action. I could use some deeper melanin in my skin. My blush is almost visible.

"What are you getting him for Valentine's Day? I think you should do something that says you love him." Kassiah sits down, her legs bouncing uncontrollably. "I know this is about you but I am so excited. I have been waiting for this moment."

I roll my eyes. "Well, I reached out to one of my professors in college to see if he can get me courtside seats for the game. He said he can do me something better, so I'm waiting for that."

One of the things I liked about being a social butterfly in my classes is that I made a lot of connections with a lot of people. I know photographers, musicians, people who work in the sports world, etc. This particular teacher was my advisor who was not really the best teacher but he always said I owe you one. When he knew he messed up classes or that one time he forgot to give me one of the classes that I absolutely needed.

"That's cool, let him watch his favorite team in New York?"

I wince. "Not favorite team, more like player."

She stares blankly before tilting her head. "So, what else do you have?"

I turn toward the closet and pull out two gift bags in red with white tissue paper. "Rosen likes to collect watches, so I got him a watch at this jewelry store downtown." I smiled when I saw it, and instantly knew that was the one for Rosen. He loves a good watch. It's one of the things I always get him that I know never goes out of style.

"I also got him something sentimental but I'm waiting for that to be delivered. But I got him a tie, and a few other things in that bag."

Kassiah looks in the bag and back at me. "I think he will like all the things you give him."

"I planned something for us when we get back home, too." I smile, thinking of all the plans. I feel as if I'm turning into Rosen a little bit.

"Look at my sister, all in love." Kassiah wipes a fake tear from her eye before laughing at the frown on my face.

"Come on, Star is waiting for us to pack." I grab her hand and drag her up the steps to find Star sitting in my suitcase.

"What are you doing, little one?" I laugh. "You don't think you can fit in there, do you?"

She laughs. "It was worth a shot."

Our plane leaves at 5 tonight, which means to be ready by 3:00 because of all the luggage checks and the lines. Rosen will probably get here around 2:00, which gives me plenty of time to think of something else to get him for Valentine's Day. Do men like flowers? I got him a card, and a bear. I even got him a gift basket sent to the hotel once he sent me the details. I pray that my professor can come through with the tickets. I know how much Rosen likes basketball, professional and college. He even collects figurines of his favorite basketball players. I just hope it's all enough.

I wonder if that's how he feels. If all this is enough. Will I like the moments with him? I know he would appreciate takeout dinner and everything, but I need this to be perfect.

After packing and google searching some things in New York, Rosen arrives at 2:30, just as expected. I bring my bag to the door and open it, seeing a glowing Rosen.

He smiles when he sees me and takes my bag. "Are you ready to go to New York? I heard there's a big bookstore out there. We can check it out if you want."

I smile. "I'd like that. I also was searching around and saw that your favorite basketball player, Iverson Smith, is having a signing tomorrow at a local sporting goods store; maybe we can check it out." I try to sound nonchalant as If I was not excited by this local revelation. Thank God for a quick search and social media.

"Hell yeah, I would like to check it out." He smiles. "We got time to spare before the event tomorrow, we can check out whatever you like."

He loads my bag into the car and we head straight for the airport. It isn't until I see the flying contraption that I remember how much I hate planes and heights. My mom would have me stay up all night and pop melatonin before the plane took off, so I could sleep when we headed across the country to see my Uncle Randy in California. I forgot to stay up and I don't think I have melatonin.

Rosen holds my hand as we wait in the line to board. I give his hand a tight squeeze as we walk through what feels like a metal box to get on. "You'll be sitting next to me, right?"

"I won't have you sitting by yourself. We'll be in first class, anyway."

I snap my head at Rosen, who chuckles at how dilated my pupils got.

"My boss booked the flights, don't worry." He looks down at my hand, seeing my knuckles almost turn white from the grip. I can see a look of concern in his eyes as the line starts to move. We finally board the plane and find our seats once we are able to get past the stragglers who take forever to put away luggage.

I sit in the window seat as Rosen puts away our luggage. I breathe in slowly, closing my eyes to pretend I'm on a train or something.

Rosen tilts my chin to face him, and my eyes flutter open. Rosen connects his forehead with mine, I close my eyes again, taking in the smell of his masculine cologne, the minty freshness blowing from his full lips.

"I know you don't like planes, but I'm here." Rosen says.

Rosen softly kisses my forehead. I lay my head on his shoulder and try my best to fall asleep.

"Wake me up if we start to crash." I joke.

I feel the rise and fall of his shoulders as he laughs. "Sure thing, princess."

***

### *Rosen*

I stayed up all night perfecting the last minute preparations for Kayani's Valentine's Day surprise, and by the looks of it, she's been trying to make sure that I have a surprise as well. Once we take the short flight to New York, a driver waits for us in the taxi area. My name is plastered on a white sign. We roll our bags up to the driver, who smiles when he sees us.

He immediately takes our bags and exchanges quick hellos. He must have other clients to get to today. I open the car door for Kayani and follow in behind her, smelling the cherry car fragrance.

We sit in silence, letting the soft hum of the engine soothe us as we stare at New York as it prepares for the evening.

"You want to go to Times Square tonight?" I ask as we drive through the city. She nods, resting her head against my shoulder. Lights start to shine on the buildings as the sun sets on the New York skyline. We arrive at our hotel, the building tall in the sky, a white-gold color scheme that's meant to scream 'Only people with Money stay here'. I tip our driver and wait for him to grab the bags out of the car.

Once checked in, I let Kayani shower and change first before doing so myself. I walk out of the bathroom in my gray sweatsuit. Looking at the spacious hotel room, it almost feels bigger than my first apartment. There's a comfy sitting area on the other side where an open kitchen is as well. There's only one bedroom, so on the other side of the room is a balcony with a heated pool. This space will work perfectly.

"You ready to go to Times Square?" Darkness coats the sky now, lights from the buildings twinkle the sky, creating the perfect scenery for a walk.

"What's in Times Square?" She slips on her boots and coat and walks over to me. She looks up into my eyes and a sparkle is mixed into her perfect pupils. She looks tired, a hint of bags forming under her eyes, which I wish I could kiss away.

I chuckle as I put my coat on, feeling uneasy by the stare of Kayani's big eyes. "Promise me you don't judge?"

She smirks, fighting back laughter. "I feel like you're going to tell me something crazy." She twists her mouth in her hands to stop herself from cackling.

"I didn't say what I wanted to say yet and here you go." I shake my head as I zip up my coat.

"I'm sorry, tell me." she says.

She's quiet, her expression blank as she waits for my response. I let out a little sigh, feeling self conscious.

"Well, on Social media I always see those people dancing, sort of wanted to see them."

She smiles, a little giggle escaping her lips. "Were you hoping to join them?"

"No, but I was hoping you would, Ms. Influencer."

She shakes her head. "I did bring my tripod in case we hit some book-stores."

"We definitely will check out some book stores." I wrap my arm around her shoulder and walk toward the door, our steps falling in tandem as we head toward the lively city of New York.

As soon as the cold air hits my body, I instantly wish I had gloves. I pull Kayani closer to me when I feel the shiver run through her body.

"Don't worry, beautiful, I will warm you up." I rub her arm, I can see my frosty breath as I speak the words to her.

She looks up at me instantly. I tilt my head. "Do you not know you are beautiful?"

"You surprise me everyday." I can see some of the lights in her eyes. They twinkle and dance as she stares back into my eyes.

"Why do you say that?" I ask her.

"You just do."

We walk through the slow foot traffic of New York, looking at the bright lights and feeling the cool air. Even in the dark, there is still heavy foot traffic. I read that there was a mini winter market somewhere close by and I plan on stopping by, but first I need to see these dancers.

A guy with a coffee cart stands on the corner just ahead. I buy two cups of hot chocolate and give the guy a ten dollar bill, not caring for the change. Kayani and I walk closely together, both of our hands holding our cups of hot chocolate to warm our gloveless fingers.

"I can buy us gloves if I find a store that sells them." I take a sip of my hot chocolate, the liquid warming my body and slightly burning my tongue.

"I think that would be a great idea."

I stare at the paleness of Kayani's face and frown. "Yeah, let's get you a hat and scarf, too."

Kayani touches her hair when I mention the hat but she looks super cold. Winter does not do our melanin justice. I put Kayani's hood over her head and pulled her as close as possible, hoping to radiate some body heat to her.

"Rosen, my hair." She rolls her eyes.

"You'll be doing a different style for the party anyway, you always do." I shrug, which earns a half smile half frown from her.

"Whatever." Her smile wins through her fake frown. I wouldn't be surprised if she is thinking of her next hairstyle for tomorrow.

We eventually find a little shop, a CVS, which thankfully had our winter necessities. We downed our hot chocolate and put on our new winter hat and gloves. I felt unbelievably warm in the scarf and hat; It felt like I was trapping the warmth of the hot chocolate.

As we continue to walk through the city, Times Square gets even brighter, with the multiple billboards and screens illuminating every building and street. I can see why New York barely has street lights. People just walk and stand around looking at building boards. Some mini stands are still open, selling Valentine's Day related merch, snacks or hot chocolate. I pull Kayani toward me as we walk up to a forming crowd.

"Are we near the dancers?" Kayani asked, a little bit of excitement in her voice.

"Not quite." I couldn't hide the sliver of disappointment when I see people standing around, listening to a guy sing with his guitar. The sight seems no nice, like a free concert. People record and a few couples smile and cheer when he hits the high note of the song.

"He sounds really good." Kayani says, trying to see over the peoples head in front of her.

"I know, he does sound really good." I look over to the left of the pile and see another crowd starting to form. I smile and grab Kayani's hand.

"I think I just found what I was looking for."

She laughs as I drag her to the other side of the street. Where, to my luck, a curly headed boy and a little girl dance to low trending music in front of the camera man.

"Do you want to get into the video frame so you can see yourself in the video later?" Kayani asks.

I shake my head. "No, the last thing I need is for clients to see me in a video like this." I chuckle at the thought, remembering the viral vacation video of one of my coworkers taking a shot glass out of a waitress's chest with his mouth. The clients saw that video and didn't want someone like that handling their money. As if they can have a say in what we do with our money.

"Your boss is so stuck up that nobody can dance?"

"I can dance." I shrug. "The song just has to be appropriate."

She nods her head. "Would dancing offend the client that you have to go see tomorrow? Didn't you meet with him this week? What's he like?"

I did meet with this client recently for lunch. It was the one I took Kayani to yesterday, actually.

"He's a stick in the mud who thinks he is a fun guy, but he isn't." I shrug, my attention getting lost in the dancers in front of me. "I don't think he would like me dancing with music that talks about sex and drugs."

"What is this event for anyway?" Kayani shifts her weight on one leg, her eyebrows rising questionably.

"The event is for some type of charity. I don't know, but that's what I think, the boss didn't tell me much. He just said to get on his good side, the guy is loaded."

"I don't think I could do what you do. Work is hard enough as it is." Kayani shakes her head. "You can't even dance in public."

"I can dance, I just have to be careful. One wrong post and I'm screwed." I can't help but think of that poor guy again. He now works in a division under us that works with regular people like college professors, old ones who aren't on any social media.

Kayani laughs and turns her attention away from the dancers. "I'm sorry but that doesn't sound fun. Your image has to make the company money, too? What happened, I thought you wanted to be like a sports agent or something."

I sigh. "If I can show that I can manage money then I can do just that. This is only a step in the right direction. Plus there are sports clients who work with us. I just need to keep networking and impressing the boss, and maybe he'll throw me a bone."

Mr. Harbough knows that I have a want for sports. Instead of playing basketball, I wanted to be in the stadium all the time, my hope was to work for my favorite team back at home.

"You know, I think you're very close to reaching that goal." Kayani slips her gloved hands into mine, what I wouldn't give to feel her skin.

"Just because you said that, I believe it."

She pulls me away from the crowd a little bit, a new dance song coming onto the speakers behind us. She lets go of me, smiling before hitting the dance in front of me. In sync with the dancers in the crowd.

I howl with laughter as she smiles, continuing the dance before the song stops playing. "I could be a dance influencer, too." She rocks her hips to the new beat playing.

I grab her hips and pull her close to mine, pressing my forehead against hers. "Promise me you'll dance at the party like that." She grabs my face, a smile brighter than the lights, her warm, sweet smelling breath blowing on my face. "I can't make any promises, but I'll try."

We sway out in the open, two different harmonies playing on either side of us but it didn't matter. We dance to the melody of our heartbeats in sync.

# Chapter 9

*Rosen*

Would you believe me If I said I was nervous? Today is February 14th, and while the day is going smoothly, I'm still nervous for what is to come later. The real surprise.

Kayani holds my hand, leading me through the bookstore, her tripod in front of her recording the scene before she goes absolutely crazy in here. I just hope she has room in her bag. We just came back from the signing. Since it was a little farther away from the bookstore and hotel, we decided to hit the bookstore on the way back. I got my signed jersey, Kayani bought me one at the store before I stood in line, and got my picture with my favorite player. Eight year old me would wear that jersey and never take it off. Twenty-three year old me is going to have this framed on the wall until I get a man cave.

We walk through the huge bookstore, recording every floor and the sections. I can get used to Kayani in her element, the way she looks at the design layouts in certain areas and the displays, scoping out the types of books she wants for her own bookstore. The way she moves fluidly as if she's been here before. Kayani in her natural element is truly a beautiful sight to see.

"Let me take that tripod from you so that way you can get some books."

She turns back to me and smiles before stopping her recording and handing the tripod to me. I hold her in frame as she looks around the bookstore.

"I want to go to romance and then the fantasy section and then fiction." She says, interlacing her hand with mine again and leading me toward the second floor.

"About to go crazy in here, I see." I laugh

She turns back to me, shaking her head. "I think I'll just get three, one from each section."

I frown a little bit. "Get as many as you want, think of it as a part of your gift."

This morning, Kayani woke up to flowers and a gift card for a small bookstore back home that I had gotten a while back. It was supposed to be for her birthday, but I found it while packing.

"Are you sure? I don't think I have enough room in my suitcase."

"I got room."

Once we hit the second floor, she stares at me, as if trying to see if I am calling bluff.

"Any book you want, princess. Grab 20 if you want."

I press record on her phone, earning a huge smile as I follow her to the romance section. She grabs 3 books, all a part of a series, I'm guessing, from the similar covers. And a book on display with color designs.

"Rosen, I think I might just get romance, and get fantasy later." Her eyes are fixated on the titles as she walks slowly down the aisle.

"Get whatever books you want."

She smiles and grabs a few more books. I hold onto the books with my free hand, wishing I grabbed a basket. We walk to the fantasy section, which thankfully, she grabs only two books.

"That looks interesting." I say, looking at the purple flames and girl with wild curly hair.

"It just came out a week ago."

"I might read that while you get ready." I chuckle

"It's not going to take me forever to get ready."

I check the time. 1:00 p.m. and I planned to take her to get lunch before we head back to the hotel to get ready for the event.

"Listen, you might do an elaborate skincare routine, try on about 8 dresses and ask me how you should wear your hair."

She rolls her eyes. "I would not do that."

"You did before." I shrug.

"That was an important banquet for my degree." She holds her finger to me like a knife.

I grab her finger and place a gentle kiss on the back of her hand. "It was important and you looked beautiful."

Kayani wore a gold dress that night and had her hair in an updo. We took a picture together that sits on my parent's fireplace in a frame. It's one of my favorites

She looks away to hide the discoloration on her cheeks and walks with me toward the register. After paying for the books, Kayani and I walk to the hotel, looking at the displays, window shopping all the way back.

Are you ready for lunch?" I ask as we head into the building, getting onto the elevator. Kayani yawns slightly.

"I think I'll have a nap, rest for tonight." She takes one of the bags from me. "But you can grab me a little sandwich or something."

I nod as the elevator opens up to our floor. I grab Kayani's hand, leading her to our room and setting her bag of books on the table. She pulls out her books and phone to take some aesthetically pleasing shots.

"I'll let you do that and I'll find us some food."

She nods, a wide yawn overcoming her face. "You do that. I may be asleep by then."

I chuckle and grab the room key. "I'll see you when I get back, princess."

"Rosen," Kayani calls, followed by a huge yawn. I almost want to crawl in bed with her and nap myself. But I need something filling, especially if the food at this event is nasty.

"Yes, Kayani." I pause with my hand on the door handle.

"How come you call me Princess all of a sudden." Her voice is drenched with exhaustion. I can only picture her eyes fluttering open every couple of seconds to fight her sleep.

"You're not my queen yet." I smile to myself, thinking of the surprise I have planned later. I pause, waiting for Kayani's response.

"Kayani?" I call out to her, only to be met with the sound of soft snores. I chuckle softly and move over to Kayani, giving her a gentle kiss on the forehead before I officially walk out of the door.

"See you later, princess."

***

### *Kayani*

Rosen isn't here when I wake up, Which is perfect for me to start getting ready for tonight. My stomach rumbles, sending warmth through me as hunger courses through my body. I wonder what kind of appetizers they'll have at the event tonight.

I pull my suitcase from under the bed and pull out my skincare bag. I walk towards the bathroom just as the soft clicks of the door open up signaling Rosen's return. I peek my head out of the room and see him with a rose and a bag of food that smells heavenly.

"Sorry it took me so long. I was in the mood for chicken sandwiches. I found a spot but traffic was wild." He places the bags in the living area and walks over to me to give me a forehead kiss and throw his key on the dresser.

My heart knocks against my chest, feeling his lips against my skin. "About to do extensive skincare, huh." He chuckles as he takes off his shoes and lays back on the bed.

"Not until after I eat." I say, my breath airy.

I walk over to Rosen, putting my skin care down and crawling on top of him, sitting on his lap. His eyebrows raise, intrigued as he puts his hands on my waist, sending shivers through my body, feeling his cold hands.

"Your hands are cold." I place my hands on top of his as he smiles.

"Your skin is warm." A new look forms in his eyes. He licks his bottom lip before sitting up, pulling me closer to him. I can hear my blood flowing through my veins as my heart pounds rapidly.

"You ready for tonight?" He snakes his arm around my waist, his voice dangerously low.

"I mean." My tongue is dry, the only thing that I can think about is his hands on my body. My body stiffens as he gets closer to me. His body heat radiates to me as his cold hands rub my waist.

"I'm a little nervous, I just hope that I brought something pretty to wear tonight."

He pauses, his mouth close to my ear, "Hold that thought." He moves me off his lap, which I frown at, but I quickly fix my face when he turns to me. He fights his smile as he stares at me. He opens the closet door, feeling around blindly for an item. He pulls out a dress cover from the closet and places it gently on the bed.

"I thought you would say something like that."

I open up the cover to see the beautiful purple dress from the boutique Rosen and I visited the other day. I place my hands over my heart. "Rosen, you didn't."

"I had to," Rosen chuckles.

"Because it's the shade of purple that you like on me?" I smile, holding up the dress to my body.

I feel his presence behind me as he snakes his hands around my body. "Eat up and get ready so we can get out of here." He places his chin on the top of my head. We stay there for a minute, looking out at the New York skyline. What I wouldn't do to kiss his lips and tell him I love him. If only I wasn't scared.

His hands slip away from my waist, his footsteps getting softer each growing second. I stare in the mirror and hold the dress over my body with a smile that won't go away.

***

"I know you'd rather spend your Valentine's Day another way. But I just want to thank you for being by my side."

I grab Rosen's hand, giving it a tight squeeze as we stand outside the building of the event. We walk to the front of the building, a man holds the door open for us as we enter the space. So many men in suits but none of them compared to Rosen.

A man in a dark blue suit comes up to Rosen, his bald head shining under the fluorescent lights.

"Rosen." He says cheerfully, giving Rosen a quick hug. "It's a pleasure for you to be here." His smile is wide, making a crinkle form at the edges of his eye

"It's nice to be here Mr. Dean." He holds out his hand for him to shake, which he accepts. He catches my eye and nods his head.

"Who is your friend? You bring pretty ladies to my event and not introduce me, or grab her a flute of champagne." He motions to the waiters around the building carrying trays of hors d'oeuvres and champagne flutes.

"Sorry, Mr. Dean." Rosen begins before Mr. Dean cuts him off.

"Please, Rosen, call me Josh. I think we earned our way past the last name basis. I don't call you Mr. Green."

Rose nods, a tight lipped smile on his face. "Yes, sir. Anyway, this is Kayani, she's my date for the night.He nods, giving me a once over. "You did a good job bringing her here on Valentine's Day."

Rosen's spine straightens as he pulls me a little closer to him. "Can't go anywhere without my girl. You know the feeling."He nods. "Of course. Please mingle, help yourself to some food."

Rosen nods his head as Josh walks past to greet the next person.

"So glad I don't have your job." I say as I hold onto Rosen's arm, the intoxicating scent of his cologne makes me want to be closer to him than I already am. We walk through the spacious room, grabbing champagne flutes and as many crab appetizers as possible.

I talked myself into a social battery drain. I felt small talking to most of the women here, as they talked about some businesses they invest in and companies their husbands own. I chimed in a few times when asked about what I do, trying to make my bookstore and influencer jobs sound interesting.

After my second champagne flute and 10th crab appetizer, I walk over to Rosen, who talks to Josh and two other men. He looks more natural than he did before. He laughs at the jokes, I can tell by the twitch of his hands and the tone of his voice, he's only pretending and desperate for a get away.

I walk up to Rosen, a big smile on my face, "Hi gentlemen, do you mind if I steal Rosen for a second."

The men shake their heads and raise their champagne glasses to me. "Be my guest."

I take Rosen away and once he is out of ear shot, he lets out a sigh of relief. "Thank you for that, Princess."

I smile, "I thought you could use a break."

He takes my half full champagne flute and downs the rest of my drink. "Enjoying yourself?" I ask. He looks around the room.

"I don't enjoy talking to these people on my off days." Rosen chuckles. "But, tell me. Are you enjoying yourself?"

"Absolutely not. I think those women over there were going to throw up when I said I owned a bookstore."

Rosen looks me up and down. "I think they're just shocked that you own a bookstore. With that dress, they're thinking more."

Rosen wets his bottom lip, lust twinkles a little in his eye. I think he's not the only one thinking more.

"When are we getting out of here?" I walk up closer to him, a slither of space between our bodies. I can breathe and feel the fabric of his suit against me.

"Now, if you want." Rosen's voice deepens, sending a shiver down my spine.

I nod, unable to speak words. Rosen grabs my hand and walks over to Mr. Dean to say goodbye, and he mentions that he will contact his office soon. From the triumphant smile on his face, I can tell that Rosen accomplished what he should have tonight. One step closer to his dream.

Rosen hails a taxi, which we take back to the hotel. I feel stuffed off the drinks and small bites I had. One more and I might tear this dress. I can't wait to get back home to lift weights again.

"So, would you come with me to work trips more often? I could use the company." Rosen says as the Taxi pulls up in front of the building.

"I would, actually. Even if they are a little boring."

Rosen fakes the offense. "My job isn't interesting enough for you?"

I mush his face. "Not in the slightest."

A wild grin appears on his face when he turns his attention back to me. "It was better with you at my side, though."

The driver rolls his eyes as he pulls up in front of the building. I laugh, which catches Rosen's attention.

"Don't get mad because you don't have any game." Rosen hands the man his money and helps me out of the car. We laugh our way into the building.

Rosen stops in front of the elevator. "I know this isn't the day you're expecting." The doors open as a couple steps out of the elevator dressed to the nines

"I always have fun with you, though, Rosen; we can order take out and watch a movie." I pause a little bit, "Cuddle?" The last words coming shaky out of my mouth.

He smiles. "I would like that."

We step onto the elevator, riding up to our floor and back to our hotel room. "Ladies first." Rosen says as he motions for the door.

I swipe my card and open the door, a sight every girl dreams of rests before me. Rose petals and candles light the floor. I stand speechless, my mouth hanging open for dear life.

"Keep going." Rosen whispers into my ear. I continue to walk to the bedroom, the rose petals flowing, soft music playing in the background. As I open the door, more rose petals litter the floor, heart balloons surround the ceiling, multiple gift bags fill the bed, and bouquets sit on each dresser. Balloon letters of 'Will you be mine?' float right in front of the balcony window.

"Rosen." I say breathlessly, looking at the decorated space. I open my mouth to speak but words are impossible.

"Tell me. Does this feel like a chapter from your stories?"

He stands blurry in front of me as tears fill my eyes. "I don't know what to say." I turn to the flowers, a single rose in a case rests in heart shaped flower petals on the bed.

Rosen presses his body against me. With a swift move of my hair, he places a rose gold necklace over my heart.

I turn my body, the back of my knee pressing into the mattress. Rosen grabs the rose case on the bed and hands it to me. "I hope I'm able to make you forget every bad encounter you had on this day, beautiful. I hope that you can replace those with thousands of days with me." He uncaps the case, showing one single rose, a deep red hue. "Let me show you that roses will always be red with me."

I grab the rose and place it on the bed and take his face in my hands. Our lips crash, the sweet taste of Rosen is what I've been desperate for, ever since that night on my porch. The day I deemed a mistake, but the only mistake was not telling Rosen how I felt.

We part breathlessly, our chests rising and falling in sync. "Rosen, I love you, I have always loved you, and It didn't take me this week to figure it out. I always have, I don't want to go a day without letting you know that."

He smiles, pressing his forehead against mine. "Can you tell I love you, too?"

I laugh and peck his lips again and again. "Absolutely."

# Epilogue

"Come on, what kind of call is that, Ref." Rosen screams at the ref who stands just a few feet away from us.

I laugh, seeing Rosen hyped up, he wears a brand new Jersey that he bought just to rep his team tonight. He looks down, smiling at me. The rest of his gifts are still at my house.

"I hope you know that I could propose to you right now, this is the best seat I've ever had." He sits back in his chair and eats out of my popcorn bucket.

"I was hoping you liked them." I place my head on his shoulder and watch as number 28 makes free throws.

Rosen grabs my chin and kisses my lips, "I love you." He says, staring into my eyes. I peck Rosen's lips multiple times, earning a smile before turning my attention back to the game. He grabs my hand, squeezing it gently.

"You think your mom will be hype when she finds out we're finally together?"

Rosen nods. "Yup, she'll be ecstatic after she sees this." Rosen points to the jumbotron, our face popping up for the kiss cam.

I grab Rosen's face, the softness of his beard between my fingers as I place a kiss on his lips. The crowd cheers as if we won the game. When in reality, I won this game we call love.

# Acknowledgements

First and foremost I want to thank God. This book would not be published if it was not for Him blessing me with this talent. Life has a weird way for inspiring this book. Of course, I wanted to live my hopes out through Kayani and for everyone that has ever felt like this, who never had a proper Valentines Day. It's okay, we will have one eventually.

Special thanks to my twin sister Christina for always rooting for me and for my book besties. You all keep me going. Thank you to my editor for this novella Marked By Tylee you are the best. Also, I cannot forget my cover designer Mireia! You're a great artist

You all deserve a happily ever after and I hope you are blessed with one.

# About the author

Ciana Smoak is an educator by day and an author by night. When she is not writing cute YA and NA romance novels, she can be found crocheting stuffed animals, singing her heart out to old school R&B, and reading books.

You can connect with her on TikTok at Cianasmoak2 and Instagram at Ciana.Smoak

# Also by Ciana Smoak

Single and Crochet comes out this Spring.